BARDSONG

Glimmer Vale Chronicles #7

MICHAEL KINGSWOOD

CONTENTS

ABOUT THIS BOOK

Julian, Melanie, and Jared have returned to Lydelton. And not a moment too soon. Snow has begun falling in the passes, and soon no one will be able to travel in or out of Glimmer Vale and its environs unit the spring thaws arrive.

But other new arrivals have made unexpected changes in the town they remember. And as strange, almost mystical, events begin to unfold around them, the re-united team will need all of their wits and skill to get to the bottom of it all.

Bardsong is the seventh novel in the Glimmer Vale Chronicles, a fun and exciting mystery set in a world of valor and magic.

Enjoy the book! After you're done, please come to Michael's website and sign up for his mailing list at www.michaelk-ingswood.com/newsletter-signup/. Guaranteed to be spam free, he uses it to announce new releases and special promotions for his fans.

MAP OF GLIMMER VALE

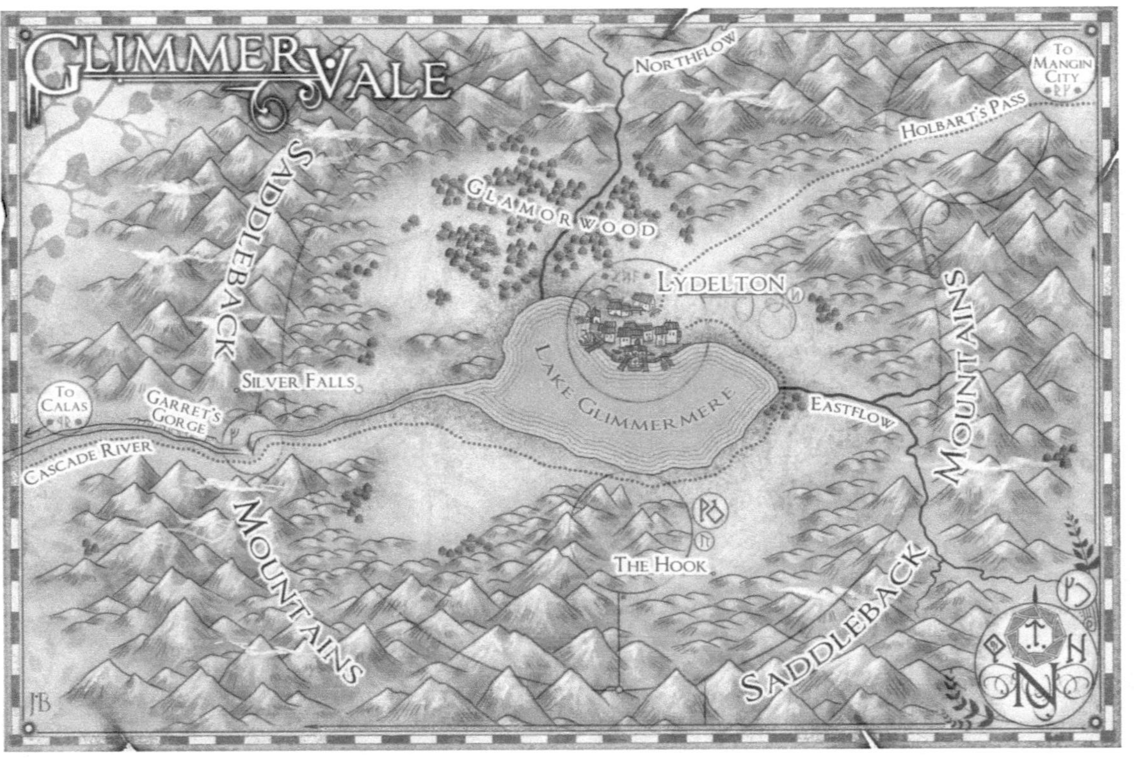

GLIMMER VALE
Northflow
To Mangin City
Holbart's Pass
Saddleback
Glamorwood
Lydelton
Mountains
Silver Falls
To Calas
Garret's Gorge
Lake Glimmermere
Eastflow
Cascade River
Mountains
The Hook
Saddleback
N

COLD RETURNS

The whistling of the wind past the walls of the Constabulary drew Raedrick Baletier's eyes away from the report he was finishing and over toward the building's stout, and firmly shut, pine door.

Pine, like the rest of the building. But the door was stained a darker color than the walls, floor, and ceiling. Those were more pale, barely stained at all in truth. But it was well put together, the gaps between the planks of the walls well-sealed and the space between the inner wall and the outer structure insulated with… well, Raedrick wasn't sure what with.

He knew for a fact the men who built it, like all the other structures in Lydelton, had insulated it somehow. But in spite of that he felt the chill seeping in from outside. Only the cast iron wood stove that sat in the corner across the room from his desk, adjacent to the desk Julian normally used, kept his office close to comfortable.

The cell block, extending from a barred door between his desk and Julian's didn't have that benefit. Oh, there was a small stove at the rear of the space, but it wasn't nearly enough to heat the half-dozens cells back there much at all.

For some of the miscreants he had locked up in there since he came to town almost two years ago, Raedrick wouldn't have felt too much sympathy. But the man back there now, huddled beneath a pair of thick wool blankets on his cot in the middle cell on the left, was different.

Trevir wasn't a bad man, just a man who had his world collapse around him. An errant word from one of his fellow fishing men on their boat had sparked an inferno within him, and he'd lashed out.

Fortunately, Raedrick had been able to talk him down before he did any real harm, aside from a cut to Gilroy's leg. But still, Trevir had an appointment with the judge. Raedrick had expected a light sentence, pressed for it, actually. But whether because he wanted to set an example, or because of the fishing company's importance to the town's—and really the entirety of Glimmer Vale's—economy, or because he'd just gotten up on the wrong side of the bed, the judge had rejected that notion.

So Trevir had to spend the rest of the month in Raedrick's cell block, on top of the fine the judge imposed.

Not outside of the requirements of the law; in fact the judge could have gone much more severe. But as he listened to the wind outside and looked back toward the closed door to the cell block, Raedrick couldn't help frowning in dissatisfaction.

Trevir had three children and a wife—an unfaithful wife, it turned out, which is what had set him off—to care for. He couldn't do that in a cell, not very well, anyway.

Fortunately, Horace, the head of the fishing guild, had arranged with the Covington Brothers to pay their fishing men year-round, not just during the months when they were actually out on the boats. So Trevir's family would have some money coming in. But…

A particularly strong gust whipped around the building, and Raedrick frowned over at the wood stove again, but really at the empty desk next to it.

And that was the real source of his pique today, he realized.

The weather had finally begun to turn, Glimmer Vale's short

autumn collapsing into the frigid cold that would grip the high elevation community for the next five months. There hadn't been any appreciable snowfall…yet. But the first dusting had fallen just yesterday.

Raedrick snorted. Dusting. Where he grew up, in the lowlands well east of the Saddleback Mountains that housed the vale, what was deposited yesterday would constitute a heavy fall.

Here…not so much.

Still, hearing the wind blow, and knowing the rapidity with which winter was coming on, as he looked at the empty desk he could not force down concern that was rapidly growing into full-on worry.

Julian Hinderbrook, his partner in the Constable's position, had embarked on a journey out of the vale with Melanie Klemins and Jared Tolburt months ago, before spring had fully turned into summer. From the distance they had to cover to get to The Falconer's Stairs and back, they should have been back long ago.

Unless something had gone wrong.

Several times over the last couple months he'd considered sending a pigeon down to Caperick Leminster, one of the Royal Marshals posted in Mangin City, the first city to the east of the Saddleback Mountains, to inquire if he'd seen or heard from them and perhaps ask him to send out a search party.

But he'd held off. The place they were going had been lost for five hundred years or so, and no one else knew about the treasure hidden there. And he really didn't know where to tell Leminster to look.

There was also the fact that Melanie wasn't supposed to leave the Vale, by agreement with Vigilant Haversted of the Magestirium in exchange for them not pressing charges against her for unlawfully practicing magic.

So he really hadn't wanted to draw official eyes toward their expedition, for her sake.

But now he realized that was a mistake. The weather had turned and they were not back yet. Very soon the pass through the mountains to Mangin City would be impassable, if it wasn't already—the mountains' snowpacks had already visibly increased and indications were the pass had already seen a fair amount of snow even if they hadn't here in the Vale…yet. So they would be stuck in the lowlands if they hadn't already made the journey. Or if they had attempted the pass they might be in dire peril now.

There were still pigeons in the town's hutch. Perhaps he should send one to Leminster now, before the weather got worse. And he ought to talk with Povol, one of the local mountaineers. He could lead an expedition into the pass to see if they were laid up there…

Raedrick snorted again. Foolishness.

Julian could be impulsive but he was no fool. Neither was Melanie. They wouldn't attempt the pass if it was clear there was no way through. So maybe they'd have to remain in Mangin City until spring. Not a big deal, was it?

And anyway, without actual information that they were in trouble, sending an expedition would most likely be a waste of time and effort, and put other people into potential harm's way without cause.

"You've got enough to worry about right here," he said softly to himself, and forced his eyes away from the stove—and the empty desk—and back to the parchment he'd been writing on.

It was time for his monthly report to the mayor, and he had the report just about done. Really he'd finished it last night, but he was reading it through one last time before their meeting at noon. It—

A gust of chill blasted Raedrick as the front door swung open and a cloaked figure stepped into the room. A few flecks of white swirled through the air around him as he paused in the doorway for a second, then he kicked the door shut behind himself.

The door latched with an audible clack and the cloaked man shrugged off a long, furred scarf that he had wrapped around his neck and the lower portion of his face. Then he turned and, doffing the cloak, hung both up on pegs driven into the wall next to the door.

Uncloaked, he stood about Raedrick's height, with shortly-cut brown hair. His coat was deep green, and smudged with dirt and soot in various places, his leggings grey-brown. His boots were thick leather and came up to his calves, and he wore a sword belt around his waist. A longsword with a hand-and-a-half hilt hung on his left hip and a shorter, curved blade on his right. As he turned back around from hanging up his cloak and scarf, he shot Raedrick a grin through three or four days' growth of beard.

"Hey, Rae," he said, and clumped over to the stove, where he held out his hands toward the warmth.

"Julian!"

Raedrick was up onto his feet and around the desk almost before he realized what he was doing. Then he was over next to his long-lost—or seemingly long-lost anyway—partner. He grabbed Julian by the shoulder and spun him around, almost unsure whether he was seeing things or not.

But no, he was real, and he had that semi-joking grin on his face that he almost always seemed to.

It was Julian, all right.

Raedrick pulled him in and gave him a hug—a masculine and brotherly hug. Julian flinched slightly for a second, then he clapped Raedrick on the back.

"Good to see you too," he said as Raedrick stepped back.

"You're back," Raedrick said. "What about the others? Are they—?"

Julian made a dismissive gesture. "They're fine. Melanie's gone to, and I quote, tackle the mountains of dust that she's sure has piled up in her shop. Jared's squaring things away with Molli's stablehands and seeing to his flat."

Jared. Not Tolburt. Raedrick couldn't remember ever hearing Julian use his first name, not since the last time they saw him back in their army days. Or the end of those days, at least.

"When did you get into town?"

Julian shrugged and settled down into his desk chair. "About an hour and a half ago. And not before time," he added, gesturing toward the wood stove. "It's getting positively cold our there. Big snowfall in the pass two nights ago. I thought we were going to turn into icicles. But we made it."

Raedrick nodded slowly, still not quite believing what he was seeing and hearing. Julian had been gone for so long…that he was back, and so suddenly, was like being on one of the fishing boats during an unexpected gale and having the deck tilt out from under your feet.

Fortunately, he had never actually been out on the boats in those conditions. But he had watched from the shore this past summer when a gale swept in, saw how far over those boats heeled in the sudden wind, and cringed to think of that feeling. Wondered how the men aboard could handle it without one or all of them going into the lake and drowning.

Julian looked away from the stove back toward Raedrick's side of the office and raised an eyebrow. "What's with the new desk?"

That brought Raedrick out of his thoughts of the summer storm. He looked over to the corner of the room opposite the wood stove, and grinned.

He had set up a small, lightly-stained pine desk there a few weeks ago, vacant now but outfitted with a blotter, pen, and ink jar.

"That's for Amos Melton, our new assistant."

Julian looked him askance. "Melton." He seemed to chew on the name for a moment, then his eyes widened slightly, in recognition. "The rancher?"

Raedrick nodded. "His son. His father thought he needed… direction, so he volunteered him to work for us."

"And how's that working out?"

"Alright so far." He narrowed his eyes at Julian. "Are you going to tell me about what happened to you three or am I going to have to beat it out of you?"

Julian chuckled. "That's a long story, and we all decided it'd be best to tell you this evening at dinner." He smirked. "Melanie seemed to think I'd miss a detail or two in the telling. And besides," he waggled an index finger at Raedrick, "she wants to see that daughter of yours."

Raedrick couldn't help chuckling at that. Women never could get enough of babies, it seemed. But still, he burned to hear what had happened on the companion's journey. The idea of waiting…

The clock on top of the shelf of case records next to the barred door to the cell block chimed softly, drawing his eye to it, and he shelved the annoyance that had begun to grow.

"There's no time now anyway. We've got a meeting with Mayor Holliman in a couple minutes."

He turned back to his desk, and the report he had been reading over. No time to go over it now, and anyway it was fine enough as it was. He hoped.

"Mayor…Holliman?" Julian said, confusion in his voice.

Raedrick picked up the report and looked back over his shoulder toward his friend, and grinned at him. "You've missed a lot around here as well. Come on, I'll fill you in as we go."

Julian got that semi-pouty expression that he sometimes got when he wanted to protest doing something, but just as quickly as it appeared, it vanished. He nodded and stood. He paused for a moment to rub his hands in front of the stove again, then he straightened and grabbed up his cloak from where he'd hung it.

"Let's get to it."

2

MEET THE NEW BOSS

As he followed Raedrick down Lydelton's main street toward the Town Hall, Julian couldn't help comparing it to the streets of Mangin City. Not that he'd spent all that much time there, or that he thought highly of it—the opposite actually—but compared with the tightly-packed, compressed, and more built-up buildings there, Lydelton seemed spacious, spread out.

And small.

He had visited plenty of places larger than Mangin City back in his army days. His travels had taken him through many of the Kingdoms largest cities and deep into the territory of their enemy to the west, and he'd seen plenty of places that more deserved the title metropolis than cities.

Compared with them, Mangin City was small and Lydelton positively tiny, almost non-existent.

But it had been more than two years since he'd been in a town larger than Lydelton, except for Mangin City. And the time he'd spent there during the journey to the Falconer's Stairs had left an impression on him, a feeling for how a city is.

Cramped. Stacked high. Filled with bustling humanity striving and surging en masse for a living, and maybe a tiny bit of prosperity in the clutter.

Lydelton, by contrast, was almost tiny. About a thousand adults total, and maybe the same number scattered throughout the rest of Glimmer Vale. Even here in the middle of what passed for the vale's hub of civilization the buildings were smaller, more spread out. Even the lowliest of the houses had at least a small plot of land between itself and its neighbors, and the boarding houses were only two stories tall. All boasted the steeply-sloped roofs required by the heavy snowfall of Glimmer Vale's winters, with at least one stone chimney poking out apiece.

And none of the streets were paved. Except Main Street, which was solid flagstone, quarried from the mountains east of town once upon a time until the residents realized the effort and expense was too great to complete the project for any but the one primary street that linked the key locations in the town.

The wind whipped past him, chilling him and making him clutch his cloak tightly around himself as the brief warmth from the stove in the Constabulary was driven away, and snowflakes clouded his vision, making him shudder both from the chill and from the peaceful beauty of their fall.

And as he walked, despite the bite of the cold he felt his spirits buoyed.

He had felt the lack of his adopted home during their travels, but it wasn't until just now that he realized just how much he'd really missed it.

Maybe it was from seeing the solid gait of his friend of so many years leading him down the street. Or maybe it was the familiar faces that he saw as he walked past. Faces that saw him, then did a double-take before they broke out in glad smiles of recognition as they beheld him for the first time in months.

Greeting those men and women caused their trek, normally one that would take only a handful of minutes, stretch into almost a half hour. But no matter, the meetings left him feeling a warmth that the chill of the day could not quench, and so when he finally clumped up the stained pine stairs to the Town Hall's front door, he was smiling ear to ear.

Inside was warm, positively hot by comparison with outside, and tiny compared with its brother down in Mangin City. But as Julian came within it felt like a palace, and he threw back the hood of his cloak with relish.

"Gods, I missed this place," he said as he and Raedrick stopped to doff their cloaks and hang them on pegs inside the Town Hall's doorway.

Raedrick clapped him on the shoulder. "And we've missed you," he said, then he nodded upward toward the stairs leading to the Mayor's office.

They walked up together.

The second floor landing was sparsely furnished. Just a bench outside the Mayor's office door, which stood open.

Inside was the room he'd visited so many times before. A broad desk with a swivel chair behind it before wide-paned windows looking out at the street below, and past that the expanse of the town leading down to the finger piers of the docks poking out into Lake Glimmermere, where the Covington Brothers's fishing fleet plied the trade that made up the backbone of the town's economy. On both walls on either side of the desk were bookshelves containing records of town ordnances and various civic data collected over the years. Two simply-carved pine chairs faced the desk immediately in front of it, and two more were set up on either side of the door as they entered. Directly above the windows was mounted the intricately carved and artistically stained seal of the town, crafted by some unnamed carpenter decades ago.

Behind the desk, in the swivel chair, used to sit Mayor Brimly, older than Julian and Raedrick by over twenty years, plump with grey hair and a belly that strained the coat he habitually wore no matter how informal the occasion.

Now the man behind it was younger by ten years or so, with flowing black hair that spilled down across his shoulders apparently without care. He had powerfully muscled shoulders and an equally stout chest beneath a simple white tunic that he wore unlaced at the collar.

Julian knew him, of course. He'd been on cordially professional terms with Stepan Holliman during his time in the vale before he departed on his journey, but not exactly friendly. Not that he didn't like Stepan; he'd just been a professionally competent man who kept to himself and didn't cross with the law. So Julian hadn't had reason to interact with him much, except to say hello while on his rounds.

Now he was mayor, and as Julian looked at the badge of office on the man's breast—a golden fish jumping out of the water of the lake—Julian found the sight a bit strange.

Mayor Holliman looked up as they walked in, and scowled. "You're late, Constable. I have other—"

He stopped when he saw Julian, and his eyes went wide. Then the scowl faded and turned into a welcoming smile. "Julian! When did you get back?"

"Just this moment," Julian said, and put on his best professional smile. "Good to see you, too. And congratulations, I guess." He waved at the office that Stepan now inhabited.

Mayor Holliman rose and rounded the desk. He extended his hand to Julian, and Julian forced his hand into it, hoping to get his grip settled before the former blacksmith could close his. And then winced when he found he hadn't succeeded and it felt like his hand was being crushed in the man's powerful grasp.

"Your trip was successful?" Mayor Holliman said, and released the shake after a blessedly brief squeeze.

"Successful enough," Julian said, and shook his hand as the Mayor released it, to get the blood flowing again. "It's good to be back though."

Holliman nodded. "I'm sure. And I know Raedrick's glad to have you back. The Covington Brothers made loan of some of their men to help out but he's been running ragged all the same."

Raedrick looked him askance. "I don't know that I'd say that, Mayor."

"Between your new young one and the events of the last several weeks? Yes, you have, and everyone can see it." He went back behind his desk and settled into his chair, and gestured for them to take the seats in front of it. He focused in on Julian. "I assume you'll want to take back your old position. When will you be ready to start?"

Julian shrugged. "Give me the rest of the day to get settled back into my flat, and I'll get going in the morning."

"So soon?"

"No reason to dilly dally."

The Mayor nodded. "As you wish." He pulled open the left-hand drawer on his desk and fished around inside it for a little bit, then withdrew a piece of silver from within. "You'll need this."

He tossed it toward Julian, and he caught it one-handed. It was his badge of office as constable: a silver clenched fist clutching a set of scales. He'd left it behind when he embarked on the journey with Melanie and Jared. The town wouldn't keep him on the payroll while he was away, and anyway being constable of Lydelton had no pull anywhere outside the vale, so what would have been the point of keeping it?

He turned the badge over in his hand, watching the glint of the sunlight coming in through the windows, dim beneath the overcast and slowly falling snow outside, on its various facets as it rotated.

"Funny how much you can miss such a little thing," he said, then he unbuttoned his coat to pin it back onto its place on his left breast.

Holliman looked quizzically at him, but Raedrick nodded. He understood, probably more than the mayor did. Holliman's trade hadn't been one that used any marks of status besides the quality of the goods he made. Julian and Raedrick had come from the army, with all its rank insignia and decorations, and then spent most of the last couple years as constables here, with a new insignia to designate them.

All those symbols and signs came to have meaning, become a part of you. And losing them felt like losing something real, somehow. No doubt Wil Brimly felt the lack of the mayor's badge now as he did whatever it was he was doing in retirement. Holliman would come to feel the same over time, Julian had no doubt.

The moment passed quickly though, and Holliman sniffed softly, looking back at Raedrick. "Well, let's keep this brief. You two have a lot of catch up on. So just give me the summary."

Raedrick stood and pulled out the parchment that he had been going over when Julian came into the Constabulary. He set it down on the blotter atop Holliman's desk, facing the Mayor.

"Nothing you don't already know about. I'll be releasing Trevir the day after tomorrow, but aside from that—"

Holliman's lips pursed. "What's the plan there? He can't go back to his wife, can he?"

Raedrick settled back down into his chair and shook his head. "He says he's going to get a room in one of the boarding houses. I checked with Bigsbe's, and they have an opening."

Holliman nodded, displeasure written on his face. "That is an ugly business. Do you think there's any chance of them patching things up?"

Raedrick spread his hands. "I'm not the one to ask. I do know I'll be keeping a close eye on Trevir when the caravans start back up in the spring. Don't want him starting trouble with his wife's lover when he comes back through town."

"Can't say I'd blame him if he did," Holliman said, and Raedrick opened his mouth to begin a reply but the Mayor held up a hand to stop him. "But I agree. Let's make sure the Covington Brothers put him on the evening shift come spring. He'll be sleeping most of the day, and then out on the boats half the night."

Raedrick nodded. "And I'm sure Horace can find something to occupy the rest of his time, to keep him out of trouble."

"Exactly." Holliman nodded.

Raedrick said, "I was planning to check on the winter stores this afternoon, but..." He looked over at Julian, and the Mayor nodded.

"That can wait til tomorrow, I think," Holliman agreed. "Anything else?"

Raedrick shook his head.

"Then I won't take any more of your time." The Mayor stood and came around his desk again.

Raedrick and Julian stood as well, and shook hands with him again. This time Julian managed to get his hand positioned right to avoid being crushed.

"Good having you back, Julian," Holliman said.

3

CATCHING UP

The Oarlock was packed with customers. Not so unusual for the last day of the work week, during the summer months anyway, but as the days grew shorter and colder —and as revenue from passing caravans ended for the year-- people tended to stay closer to home in the evenings.

Julian couldn't blame them for that. The early evening combined with the deep chill of Glimmer Vale's long winters made for an unpleasant combination, and people wouldn't want to spend coin unnecessarily until they were sure there would be opportunity to replenish it in the near future.

But tonight it was almost standing room only, and to blazes with the snow that was beginning to fall again as the afternoon light gave way to the brief dimness of the vale's twilight.

It hadn't been earlier, though. When he, Melanie, and Jared met Raedrick, Lani, and their new daughter, and took seats in the farthest booth from the entrance, in the rear left corner near the stairs leading up to the second level and the lodging rooms, there was just Rolf behind the bar and a couple of people at a table near the rightmost of the common room's two massive flagstone fireplaces, which were alight with cheerful—and warming—blazes.

Julian had seen Rolf briefly when they first arrived, but the burly bartender nevertheless left his post to clasp hands with him and Jared, and give Melanie a hug of greeting, then they'd all settled in.

Molli Millens, Lani's mother and proprietress of the inn, came out from the kitchens to give them a quick greeting then retreated back to her domain, promising the best meal any of them had enjoyed in ages.

And then it was just the five of them—six counting the kid.

Who quickly became the center of attention.

She was stuffed into a handled basket made from woven-together reeds lined with a thick blue woolen blanket that Lani had wrapped around her for the walk over from their flat. Her little face was round and red from the chill of the late autumn air on her cheeks, and she wore an expression of mixed confusion, amazement, and humor. Or at least, that's what Julian got from the way her mouth seem to lay constantly half-open and her blue eyes danced from point to point around her endlessly.

Amazingly, she wasn't crying, just making little snuffling noises when Lani unwrapped her and lifted her out of the basket for all to see.

"This is Celia," Lani said, with a smile that took her already beautiful face and transformed it into something out of a painting, she exuded joy so fully.

Celia's hair was a few shades darker than her mother's blond, and curled. Thank the gods she had her mother's nose and not Raedrick's. But he stood out more in the rest of her face than Lani did. She was dressed in a white and blue smock—it was probably called something else but Julian didn't know baby terms—that left her little feet, wrapped in blue socks, dangling out the bottom.

Melanie immediately let out a little sound that was half-sigh, half-coo, and reached out for her. "Oh, she's beautiful," she said, and Lani's smile grew even more broad.

She handed the baby off to Melanie, and she cradled her close, lowering her head to make little baby sounds at her. Melanie's wavy dark brown hair seemed to engulf the child for a second, she leaned in so close.

Julian couldn't help but stare in surprise. He'd seen Melanie in all sorts of states before but never…this. She was like every other woman Julian had ever met when they were around babies. But Melanie was never like every other woman.

It was disconcerting.

It must have taken longer, fawning over the baby, than Julian thought because two of Molli's serving girls showed up at their booth with laden trays just as Lani finally got Celia away from Melanie and laid her back into her basket.

Julian found he envied the girl that cozy spot a bit. Yes, the fireplaces had the common room comfortably warm, but that wouldn't cover the walk back to his flat. The idea of instead being carried, snuggled in a nice, thick, warm blanket was quite appealing.

The scents rising from the platters the servers set down in the middle of their table roused him from that train of thought, though. Stewed fish, fresh from the last of the fishing men's catches no doubt, in a heavily-spiced sauce that promised a heady mixture of sweet and salt, along with fire, brought heavy saliva to his mouth, and he decided he didn't envy Celia after all. No doubt nursing was fun, but it couldn't possibly compare with the feast he was looking at right that moment.

"Welcome back, Constable," said the serving girl closest to Julian. Her name was Tami, and last time Julian saw her she had been slender and bubbly, a little flirtatious. He had enjoyed bantering with her, though only in fun. Now she was a bit more plump, and her belly was pushing against the fabric of the red dress she was wearing beneath her server's apron.

"Thanks, Tami," he said, unsure what to make of the changes in her until he saw the flash of lamplight reflecting off the band on her wedding finger. Then it all made sense.

He pointed at the ring. "When did that happen?"

Tami flushed slightly. "Mid summer. Elias surprised me with it; made it himself." She held out her hand to him so he could see.

Julian whistled softly. Elias had been apprentice to one of the three blacksmiths in the vale. When Julian left, word had been he was just about ready to move up to journeyman, and maybe set out on his own. If he felt comfortable enough to propose that meant he must have passed that milestone. And given the intricate designs he had placed into the ring so that it shown beautifully, so one couldn't help think it was made of something other than iron.

So maybe there were four now. Although… Mayor Holliman had been the most prosperous, but now that he had to devote himself to city work Julian imagined the others would still get more than enough business to keep a steady trade.

"Congratulations," he said, then pointed at her belly. "For both I guess."

Tami giggled and finished setting the bowls and utensils down in front of their group, then she and her colleague hustled back toward the kitchens.

"I can see we missed a lot," Jared said, and Raedrick nodded.

Raedrick nodded. "You did."

Over the next few minutes, Raedrick told the events in Glimmer Vale since they had been away, particularly the events surrounding the election of Mayor Holliman. It was enough to make Julian forget the sumptuous spices of the stew. By the time Raedrick finished, he realized he was just staring, mouth agape, his spoon left untouched in the bowl in front of him.

"That's…quite a scam," he finally said after a moment of taking it all in.

Raedrick nodded. "And nearly successful. If not for that brawl between the ladies, who knows if we'd ever have uncovered the truth."

Jared let out a low whistle, nodding agreement. Then he swallowed another scoop of stew.

"But," Raedrick said, leaning forward a bit in his chair. "I imagine that's not half as interesting as the Falconer's Stairs." He raised his eyebrows, looking almost sternly at the three of them. "Out with it. What did you find?"

Julian looked to his right, to where Melanie sat next to him and, past her, Jared. The three of them had discussed how to tell the tale. What would be the most fun?

Julian grinned and nodded to Jared. "Go ahead."

Jared returned the grin and reached beneath the table. His hand came back up holding a bulging money pouch, which he tossed so that it landed in front of Raedrick's bowl with a solid thump combined with the rattling of coins.

Raedrick raised an eyebrow. "What's this?"

"Your cut," Jared said, and gestured toward the pouch.

Looking puzzled, Raedrick pulled the pouch closer so that it sat between his and Lani's bowls, then undid the leather thong holding the pouch closed.

He pulled the pouch open, and Lani gasped in surprised shock. Raedrick looked sharply back up at them, his eyes wide. "What—? How—?" He stammered for a moment, then stopped, clearly shocked as well.

Melanie had a twinkle in her eye. "Come now, Raedrick. You've seen gold before."

"Yes, but…" He left off, gesturing at the pouch as though he couldn't believe what he was seeing.

And no wonder, it was more gold in one place than any of them had seen in their lives, Julian supposed. Except Melanie, maybe. And that was just a quarter of the prize they had taken away from their quest. Julian had had time to get acquainted with their newfound wealth. But he remembered the sheer amazed avarice he'd felt when he first laid eyes upon the gold Feirhard had left behind.

And the even larger stack that Melanie's contact in Mangin City had given them, when he exchanged Feirhard's gold for the kingdom's modern coins.

So Raedrick's reaction was understandable. Still amusing, though.

"So here's what happened," Julian said. And then they proceeded to relate the tale of their adventure at the Falconer's Stairs.

It took longer than the election story, of course, but this time Julian didn't forget to eat. They each took turns telling their portions of the story. By the time they got to the end, it felt like an hour had passed.

Raedrick blew out a breath and shook his head. "Astounding. I never would have imagined… So Feirhard had just been waiting there that whole time."

Melanie made a non-committal shrug. "Not exactly. He had been dozing, and time flows differently there, so it wouldn't have seemed like such a long time to him."

"That's also why it took us so long to get back," Jared put in, and Raedrick nodded.

"I see that." He pursed his lips. "Any idea where he went?"

Another shrug from Melanie. "No, but he said he'd been keeping an eye on me."

"That makes me nervous, to be honest. Who knows what a man like him will do."

"He won't harm me, or any of us. That I know for certain."

"How?"

Melanie looked away from him, her eyes growing distant as she clearly mulled over her words for a moment. "He is honorable."

Raedrick opened his mouth to speak, but she held up a hand to stop him.

"The liege he served may not have been. Then again we only know the stories told by the winners of that struggle. Who knows where the truth truly lies. But Feirhard himself is honorable. We… spoke, in a way…extensively while I was detained. He thinks differently from us, and doesn't view us as truly being on his level. But he doesn't hold any malice toward us. I don't think he cares about what we do or where we go at all, except for his and my common practice of the magical arts."

Raedrick nodded. "That makes sense, I suppose."

Beside him, Lani had been listening in silence, and looking at Melanie with a speculative expression on her face. Now she said, "He didn't seem to object to your being… What was he called you, a sorceress?"

Melanie shook her head. "No, it seems that a number of women practiced the art back in his day. He seemed to find the Magestirium's restriction inane." She chuckled softly. "In fact, from his words he appears to hold them in contempt as bumbling amateurs."

"That's even more scary, to be honest," Raedrick said, and Julian was forced to agree.

"Yeah we've all seen what they can do," he said, remembering back to his army days with Raedrick and Jared. "If he thinks they're half-trained…" Julian shook his head.

They sat in silence for a moment, one and all pondering that thought. Then Jared broke the silence.

"Nothing we can do about it, though." He leaned forward, tapping his index finger on the table, in the direction of the pouch. "What do you think you'll do with your cut?"

Raedrick blinked, then looked back down at the pouch. He shook his head. "I have no idea."

Jared grinned broadly. "I know what I'm doing. A house on the lake shore, bigger than Mayor Brimly's."

"And a boat to match?" Julian asked, and Jared shook his head.

"Hell no. I hate boats."

Julian snorted out a chuckle and was about to retort when noise from the other side of the common room drew his attention.

He looked, and blinked in surprise at the mass of people filling the room. He hadn't noticed them all come in, but now every table was full and every stool along the bar, with more people standing in little groups here and there.

"What is going on?" he said.

All around the common room, the various groups were engaged in conversations ranging from subdued to boisterous, bordering on rowdy. One particular group of fishing men at a table before the farther of the fireplaces from Julian's table were apparently dicing, while at the same time he saw no less than three families with children at the tables.

But no matter where he scanned, all eyes moved back toward him and his companions.

"I guess they're happy to see us," Jared said, puffing up in his seat a little bit as he noticed the same thing, and he took the thought right out of Julian's head. He grinned. "Giving us a welcome home party, eh?" He looked at Raedrick and his grin broadened.

But Raedrick shook his head. "I hate to disappoint, but they're not here for you."

"Oh?" Jared did look like he was deflating a bit, but he also looked confused.

At that moment, an exclamation went up from someone over by the bar, and then someone else let out a little whoop. Scattered claps also sounded from around the room.

Julian realized then that Raedrick was right. They weren't looking at him and his table and friends, the crowd was looking right behind them, toward the stairs leading to the rooms upstairs.

He turned in his seat, craning his head to see what had caught the crowd's attention so, and saw a man coming down the stairs.

The man was a little above average height, with golden blond hair that flowed rakishly around his face, almost to his shoulders. He had on a stylishly-cut green coat with yellow—or maybe even gold?—buttons and trim, and a ruffled white shirt beneath. His deep brown breaches were tucked into boots that were even more dark, nearly black, and shined so they reflected the lamplight easily. He was clean-shaven and wore a serious, but also open expression on his face.

On his back was slung a wooden case of some sort, large enough that it would be bulky to move around with. But it didn't appear very heavy from the way the man moved. His stride as he descended the final stair and moved forward into the heart of the common room was smooth, balanced, and agile.

When he reached the center of the room, he paused, then smiled broadly, and the clapping commenced again, but more loudly, and from a far greater portion of the crowd.

"Who is *that*?" Melanie said from next to Julian. She sounded almost breathless.

❧ 4 ❧

THE BARD

Julian looked aside at Melanie and had to do a double-take. She was watching the man who had just come down the stares like a woman in a trance; or like a girl enraptured with some pretty that she'd just discovered. And was she…flushed?

"That," Lani said, "is Hamel the Bard." She turned from watching the strange man and gave Melanie a sly, girlish grin. "He's luscious, isn't he?"

Melanie did flush then, and removed her gaze from the bard as he resumed his walk across the room. She gave Lani a rueful look but did not reply.

Beside her though, Raedrick gave Lani a nudge with his elbow. "Luscious?" he said, and raised an eyebrow. His tone was teasing though, and she giggled in response.

"Yes, he's luscious," Lani said, leaning over against Raedrick. "But you're delectable."

Raedrick nodded slowly. "That's better."

Jared snorted. Loudly. "You two are going to make me lose my dinner if you keep this up." He looked sidelong at Melanie. "You *three*, actually. Put your tongue back in your mouth, will you Melanie?"

Melanie gave a little jerk and sent a scowl Jared's way. Or tried to, anyway. But it didn't come out with as much force as one of her expressions of displeasure normally did, and Jared merely returned it with a knowing, slightly mocking grin.

"A bard, huh?" Julian said. He looked back at the man, who had resumed his stride toward a stage that had been set up on the right-hand side of the common room by the entrance. Local musicians often would play during the evenings here but now it seemed this Hamel had laid claim to it.

He bounded up the three short stairs leading up the stage and shrugged off the box on his back, setting it gently down on the stage next to a stool that was waiting there. He began fiddling with the latches on the box, and a moment later pulled out a harp. Gently curved and painted so that it almost appeared golden, it looked pretty nice.

But then, Julian didn't know harps from tree stumps. Still it seemed fancy to him.

"We had a few of their lot with our battalion, remember?" he said, looking away from Hamel to Raedrick and then Jared, who both nodded agreement. "They turned a fine tune, but so do minstrels. So why the special title? Never could figure that. Anyway," he looked back at Hamel as he settled down onto the stool and got his harp into position, "he doesn't look like all that much to make a fuss over."

He felt an elbow in his ribs and turned to see Melanie arching an eyebrow at him.

"What?"

"Don't be snide just because he's handsome." There was a teasing twinkle in her eyes, though the rest of her expression was serious. "But to answer your question, bards differ from minstrels because they are graduates of the Morested Academy."

"The what?" Lani asked.

"It's the finest school of music in the Kingdom," Melanie replied. "When I was in the capital, Timon and I attended a number of performances in their theater. To compare a bard's music with a mere minstrel's is like comparing a well-aged wine with homemade moonshine."

Raedrick nodded agreement. "He's the best harpist and singer I've ever heard. Quite luscious, actually." He flashed a grin Julian's way, and Julian rolled his eyes.

"Ok, so what's he doing here? This place isn't exactly in the cultural hub of the world."

Lani's lips turned downward slightly, and she looked back over her shoulder toward the bard, who was fiddling with the tuning knobs atop his harp. "He was with the last caravan to come through on its way to Calas. They stayed two nights and then pushed on, but he came back a few days later. Said they'd hit snow in the pass below Silver Falls and had bogged down. The caravan owner intended to push through but he didn't want to risk it, so he came back here until spring. Mother gave him a discount on his rooms if he'll play in the evenings."

"I see that's working out well so far," Jared said, and Lani nodded.

"Business normally drops in the winter, but if things keep up this way…" She left the thought uncompleted.

Julian mulled that over, and found himself frowning. That good business would be great for Lani and Molli, and the people who worked for them. But with no money from outside the Vale coming in until the next caravans in the Spring, and more of the existing money going to The Oarlock, that meant that the other businesses in town would have a harder winter than normal.

Or maybe not. Molli would have to buy more foodstuffs from the grocers's winter stocks, and from the local brewers, to keep up with her increased demand. So maybe it wouldn't disrupt the winter norm very much at all.

Time would tell.

"Well, let's have a listen to this magical harp of his," Julian said, and Melanie chuckled softly. She nudged him again with her elbow, but more gently this time, and he returned her smile.

Then he turned back to the stage, to where Hamel had finished his tuning and was now settling himself more fully onto the stool.

The bard began to play, a little arpeggio that broke through the din of conversation that had been filling the common room, soft but still there despite most of the people having focused in on him as he began preparing to play.

The harp chords were simple at first but became more complex, a counter-melody that Julian at first couldn't fully follow. But after a few seconds the dual notes plucked from the strings seemed to sing together, and he felt something twinge in the innards of his being.

There was a beauty there, a resonance, that pulled him in, and he felt himself being carried away by it. Lifted higher as the notes, in counterpoint but also in harmony, also rose.

It continued on that way for a time that he couldn't measure, lost as he was in their dynamics.

And then Hamel began to sing.

His voice was a soft baritone, making a third part to the counter-melody his fingers were evoking from the harp strings, balancing and reinforcing it so that Julian found himself enraptured, forced to attention and more by their balance, opposing yet reinforcing the whole.

He was singing words, but it was like those words were merely the trapping, the wrapping over which the meaning of the song carried straight through to Julian's soul.

Onward and upward it rose, and Julian felt the chill of the earlier day, somehow still present deep in his being despite the warmth in the common room from the fireplaces and the myriad bodies, cast away. Until he only felt warmth, well-being.

Onward and upward the song went, until it plunged down into deeper notes, Hamel's vocals leading the way down ahead of the plucking of his strings, and Julian plunged with them. Part of him wondered at the wisdom of the descent, but only a part, the rest of him flew along in the ride downward.

And then he buoyed upward, carried upon the wave of

ascending scales plucked from the harp strings as now Hamel's voice followed their ascent, and Julian felt the hairs on his arms and neck stirred as a surge went through him, energy flowing from someplace, he did not know where.

Dimly he registered Melanie's body snuggling in more closely to him as the notes carried them both higher, and he saw Raedrick and Lani doing the same. Hamel's singing reached a crescendo of feeling and heat, and Julian's soul stirred…

And then Celia began crying.

The infant's wail snapped the spell of the song, ripping it like paper, as her throat, discordant compared with the majesty of what had just been happening, intruded into the common room.

Julian felt a moment's chagrin, bordering almost on anger, as his gaze wrenched away from the bard on his stool and focused in on the child in her basket, and a sigh, almost a verbal scowl, swept through the room.

The music stopped, and Julian realized all eyes were on the baby, crying with her ignorant but innocent need, and he wanted to…

He shook his head, snapping himself back to reality, and saw that Lani was bent over the baby's basket, concern on her face but also chagrin. Beside her, Raedrick looked a mixture of embarrassment, but also irritation, and for a second Julian was sure he felt the same nigh-on anger that he himself had experienced a second before.

Then the moment was gone, and Lani was pulling Celia up to her breast. She looked around the room and saw all the eyes on her, and she flushed.

"Sorry," she said, softly but still carrying easily to the others nearby. She put on a weak smile. "She needs changing. I think… I'll…"

Then Raedrick stood. "Let's bring her home," he said, and Lani nodded.

They gathered the infant up and headed toward the door, walking past the people packing the common room, who watched them go with faces a mix of commiseration and friendly understanding. But also, somehow beneath that…resentment?

They were gone in a moment, and silence loomed in the common room briefly. Then Hamel, from his stool on the stage, chuckled.

"Children are wonderful, aren't they?" he said, nothing but good cheer in his voice.

A chuckle swept through the room, and whatever hint of resentment that Julian thought he had sensed was gone, just as soon as it came.

The door closed behind the retreating couple, and the bard said, "How about something more lively?"

Then he commenced playing a jig. Within moments, nothing existed but the song and the urge to dance. Several couples followed that urge in between tables. Jared got up. He took the hand of a serving girl who had been standing nearby, watching and listening like everyone else, and they began taking a turn.

Almost Julian thought to grab Melanie and join him, and looking aside at her he saw she would willingly go. But beneath that there was caution in her eyes, something about the smile that had come on her face that didn't seem quite right.

He leaned in and whispered, "What's going on here?"

She shook her head, and that look of caution departed as though it had never been. She rolled her eyes at him. "Good music, or haven't you heard it before?"

Julian found himself unsure how to answer, and then she was gripping his hand and pulling.

"Come on, let's dance."

5

TRAINING

Julian leaned up against the paneled wall of the space he and Raedrick had converted into a training room. It was not very large, maybe twenty feet on a side, and unfurnished except for a thick padded rug that covered most of the floor space in the center of the room, leaving just a few feet around the circumference clear. There were no windows, and a single entrance, leading back to the front rooms of the warehouse that housed the space.

The warehouse belonged to the Covington Brothers, the owners of the major fishing company in town, and the space had formerly been used as a sail and rigging repair shop. But several years back the brothers had determined that it would be cheaper to outsource that function rather than maintain the infrastructure for it, so they had discontinued that work and the space went closed up and unused until Julian discovered it during one of his rounds, early on in their tenure as Constables.

A quick talk with the brothers and an appeal to Mayor Brimly that the small outlay to lease the space would be worthwhile, and they had themselves a place to keep up their fighting skills.

The wall that Julian leaned against was bare of decoration except for a trio of lit oil lamps, equally spaced down its length.

Its opposite, though, held racks containing a number of weapons: swords and axes, their edged blunted and wrapped in wool padding to minimize the possibility of causing any real harm.

Mostly he and Raedrick used the place, but over the months since they had begun here others had come as well. Gilroy, from the Fishing Guild, who had kept up his study of the sword after the battle against the bandits that began Julian and Raedrick's time in Glimmer Vale. Guards from the various merchant caravans that came through were also welcome to use it—for a price. As were the Royal Marshals who came to town—without a fee.

And Jared Tolburt.

Right that moment, he and Raedrick stood facing each other in the center of the padded mat, Tolburt with a blunted longsword in his hands and Raedrick with a practice version of the elegant, curved blade he had inherited from Selam, another of the fishing men who had assisted in that first battle.

When Julian first knew him in the army, Raedrick had preferred the saber, and he had been magnificent with it. Changing styles to accommodate the differences in his new blade had left him awkward at best, painful to watch at worst, for a while. But now, nigh-on two years later, Raedrick was back to his old form.

It was good to see, but painful to experience, and Julian was nursing a sore side from his own time sparring with him not a few minutes back.

He hated to say it, though, but Jared was holding his own a bit better.

He advanced, flicking the tip of his longsword toward Raedricks eyes. Raedrick moved to block the attack but his arms had barely begun to move when Jared reversed the movement of his weapon, sending it down and to the left, toward Raedrick's thigh.

Raedrick's sword moved to follow Jared's, but he was a hair too slow, and he hopped backwards.

The two weapons met in the air where Raedrick's leg used to

be...but from the wince on Raedrick's face he hadn't retreated quickly enough and he at least had gotten nicked by it.

"Nice once," Raedrick said, and stepped back to disengage.

Jared grinned and retreated a step as well, bringing his sword up to a guard in front of himself.

Raedrick made a few kicks with the leg that had taken the hit, to work the kinks out, then settled down into a ready stance as well.

His eyes flicked over toward Julian for a second. "I think you're imagining things, Julian."

Then he darted forward.

Jared's eyes had moved to follow his toward Julian, and the sudden motion made them grow wide.

He retreated fast, whipping his sword to parry Raedrick's attack and then thrusting with the point.

Raedrick pulled up short and circled, grinning at the younger man as Jared moved to match his circling.

Julian shook his head. "There was something weird going on there, Rae. You're really telling me you couldn't feel it?"

"Infants cry. They create disturbances. Happens all the time." He batted aside another thrust from Jared but did not riposte, just continued his circle. "You just hadn't really noticed it before because you don't have a kid."

"And because you create so many disturbances of your own," Jared quipped. He sidestepped, getting ahead of Raedrick's circling direction, and cut at him from left to right, at shoulder level.

Raedrick elongated the step he was taking, leaning far into it and taking his head and shoulders below the arc of Jared's cut. Then he thrust with the tip of his own weapon.

Jared hopped backwards, huffing out a loud breath as he drew his gut in.

To no avail. Julian winced as he saw Raedrick's weapon get him square in the navel.

Jared stumbled backward two steps before he caught himself

from falling. He coughed, one hand leaving the grip of his sword and rubbing his belly where Raedrick got him.

Raedrick rose from the thrust, his eyebrows rising. "You ok, Jared?"

Jared nodded, and coughed again. "Give me a moment." He winced, and rubbed at his belly again. "That smarts!"

"I've been around plenty of infants before, Rae," Julian said. "I've heard them crying and seen how other people react to them. And I'm telling you, some of the people in that room were barely holding back from coming at you and Lani last night over the interruption."

Raedrick snorted. "Hogwash."

Jared paused in rubbing his belly to look between the two of them. Then he shrugged. "I dunno. It *was* pretty awkward."

"It was. Which is why we left," Raedrick said. "No need to ruin the performance for everyone." He looked back at Julian. "But I think you're overstating it."

"It was more than that," Julian said. "You didn't feel the..." He waved his hands helplessly as he struggled to come up with the words. "The music, when it rose and fell... You didn't *feel* it?"

Raedrick laughed, amusement plain on his face. "I think you just haven't heard truly good music before, my friend. It's *supposed* to do that."

Julian had to stop himself from scowling. "I know that. It's just..." He waved over at Jared. "Did you feel it?"

Jared had left over rubbing at his belly and took back hold on his sword with both hands again. He moved toward the center to rejoin Raedrick, but stopped and shrugged for a second as Julian queried him.

"I guess?" He shrugged again.

Then he surged forward, cutting toward Raedrick so quickly Julian had a hard time registering it.

Raedrick did, though. He shifted to the side and leaned, and the cut passed him by cleanly. Then he made a cut of his own, in the same direction as Jared's so that came toward his exposed side.

Jared tucked his shoulder and dropped to the pad, rolling with his momentum as Raedrick's cut passed overtop him. He sprang to his feet at the end of the roll and turned—

Just as Raedrick was cutting at him again. He barely had time to get his blade up to catch Raedrick's before he would have taken a hit to the chest.

"I just thought it was good music, and fun to dance to," Jared said as he retreated, dragging his blade down Raedrick's as he moved.

Raedrick advanced in time with him, allowing their blades to maintain contact, and for a moment Julian wasn't sure what he was—

Raedrick's sword twisted and spun, seeming to twine around Jared's, and then Raedrick popped upward with his shoulders and Jared's weapon sprang up, opening his belly completely.

Raedrick thrust again.

Julian winced as he all but felt the tip of Raedrick's weapon striking Jared in the same place as he had moments ago.

Then he felt his mouth fall open as Jared regained control over his blade and brought it down.

It struck Raedrick in the back of the neck as he was leaning in on the thrust, and he lost his footing, landing in a heap, face down, before the younger man.

His blade left his grip as he hit the padded floor, and he laid there for a second. Then he let out a low groan.

"Rae!" Julian pushed himself off the wall and started across the padding to his fallen friend, but stopped when Raedrick replied.

"I'm alright." He rolled over onto his back and looked up at Jared, a pained half grin, half grimace on his face. "Good one."

Jared just grinned at him. He let go of his sword with his right hand and stretched it out to Raedrick. He grabbed it and Jared helped him to his feet.

Moving gingerly, Raedrick rolled his shoulders and then his neck. He winced. Hard.

"I think I'm done for the day," he said. Then he bent over, picked up his discarded weapon, and walked—a bit unsteadily—toward the weapons rack. "What does Melanie think? She was there too."

Julian followed him to the rack, spinning the short practice blade he had been using earlier slowly as he walked. "She said basically the same as you, that she'd always gotten that feeling from concerts at that Academy and I was over-thinking it."

Raedrick nodded and slid his sword into its spot in the rack. "There, you see? If there was something mystical or wonky going on, she would know."

"I guess. But I can't get the feeling there's something weird there out of my head." He frowned and looked down at his weapon. Then he chuckled. "Or maybe I'm just trying to not think about how badly you trounced me today."

He slid the short sword home into the rack, and Raedrick grinned at him. He clapped Julian on the shoulder. "Reach is a huge advantage."

"True enough. But I need to get used to it. Feirhard left me that short sword, and I don't feel like turning my nose up at an Archmage's gift, you know?"

Raedrick laughed. "Fair enough. Well, let's get to inspecting the winter stores."

6

FISHY BUSINESS

The Covington Brothers's business headquarters was located two blocks up from the lake, almost to Main Street. It was a large building that was mostly warehouse, but also contained the office space that the brothers used to manage their empire.

Julian and Raedrick had been there plenty of times in the past. Mostly just as part of their rounds, but once to investigate a robbery.

It hadn't changed much in the months Julian had been away, except the bustle of activity that had marked it before was mostly gone. During the summer months, fishing men would be at work bringing their catch in from the boats while other warehouse men would see to preserving them for sale outside the Vale or distributing them to local buyers. Entire sections of the warehouse were given over to building up stores to supply the caravans making their way through the passes to Calas to the west or Mangin City to the east, complete with loading ramps at the rear of the building for easy access to the caravan wagons.

But another section was set aside for Lydelton's winter stores, and it was to this that he and Raedrick were focused today.

Julian's side still smarted from his earlier duel with Raedrick, and he could see that the back of Raedrick's neck—what was visible around the black ponytail he habitually wore—was starting to bruise up from Jared's strike.

Good thing there was zero chance of trouble here; neither of them would be up for anything too vigorous, he thought.

The front door of the building opened facing the intersection of the two streets, at the corner of the warehouse. The Covington brothers themselves—Danil and Jakob—met Julian and Raedrick there, along with Horace, the head of the Fishing Guild.

When he saw Julian approaching, Horace stepped forward and extended his hand. His grey-bearded face stretched into a broad grin that seemed to shine from underneath the grey cowl of the cloak he habitually wore even in the summer months. It was the fishing man's uniform almost; all of them wore it but Horace seemed to never take it off. Today he also had on a thick blue wool coat underneath the cloak and nearly black pants that were at least as thick, and bloused around scuffed black boots.

"Sorry I missed seeing you last night," Horace said as they clasped hands. "Had some business. But it's good to have you back, Julian." Then he pulled Julian in and clapped him on the back for good measure.

"Good to see you too," Julian replied and returned the clap. He stepped back and looked his friend up and down. "You got skinny on me."

Horace snorted. "I can still break you over my knee, boy," he said with a mischievous twinkle in his eye.

Julian chuckled. Or he meant to, but a gust of wind blew up from the lake just that moment, caught the cowl of his cloak, and blew it back. The side of his face immediately screamed in icy shock from the onslaught.

It had stopped snowing during the night after leaving only a light dusting—barely to the top of his foot—and the sky today was almost devoid of clouds except for a few high, thin characters that seemed to hover motionless above the mountains to the east. A welcome change; he didn't really want to have to transition to crampons on his boots so soon in the season. But with the departed clouds, the temperature had actually dropped. Everyone's breath was misting immediately in front of their faces, and Julian's cheeks were already numbing up.

"How about we take this inside?" he suggested, and Horace nodded immediate agreement.

Danil and Jakob were brothers, so looked remarkably similar. Danil was the older, thin with brown hair that was rapidly departing his head and a wiry mustache. Jakob was a bit taller than his brother and a bit broader of shoulder, and he was clean-shaven. But his eyes had a vacant look about them and his mouth almost seemed to hang slightly open.

He had been hit on the head real hard during the robbery last year. When Julian had left the Vale, he was still mostly bed-ridden and could barely speak. It was good to see him up and about again, but from the slack look on his face, he obviously wasn't his old self again, even now.

Might never be, poor bastard.

Danil opened the door and gestured for Jakob to go inside. It took a moment for Jakob to understand what Danil meant, and Danil had to gesture again, more forcefully this time. Then Jakob finally gave a short, halting nod and entered.

Julian followed, and found the inside of the building was not all that much warmer than outside.

Sure there were wood stoves in the corners of the long and broad room they stepped into, but the heat from those stoves didn't carry very far, so it was only slightly better than being out in the elements.

Not that the place needed to be heated. There were no workers about except for a lone fellow who was making the rounds through the space as they entered. He wore the grey cloak all the fishing men wore and was young, so young Julian wondered if he even had to shave.

He'd met the lad—of course he had, Lydelton was a small place—but when he departed on his journey last spring Faric had still been living with his parents. But eager to be out from beneath their shadow to start making his own place in the world.

Looked like he'd begun to do just that. Yet another change that Julian had missed during his time away.

"Like I told the mayor the other day," Danil said as he walked toward the nearest of the four doors at the rear of the sorting room, "everything is in readiness. Even with the loss of personnel last spring to the Royal Marshals's service and to your needs this fall," he looked at Raedrick when he said that, and raised an eyebrow. "The extra catches from the extended working season filled our stocks completely."

He pulled the door open and Julian almost had to step back.

The entire warehouse smelled of fish. Of course it did. But the room past that door positively reeked of it.

And no wonder. Bins were spaced all throughout the next room, filled with fish from the lake. They had been preserved for winter storage, but also many were getting on toward frozen, if not frozen through already.

The windows lining the right-hand and rear walls of the room were open, fine wires mounted on their exteriors in place to prevent creatures—or people—from getting within. But that also allowed the room to equalize with the frigid temperature outside.

In the summer, Julian knew, parties of men were sent on occasion into the peaks to the east, where the snowcap never melted, to collect hunks of ice. They would cart them back and deposit them here and in other ice houses throughout town to aid with food preservation, and to cool the drinks of the more well-to-do folks in town. Or really the caravan masters who passed through.

But now that winter had come upon the Vale—or near enough to it, anyway—those expeditions were no longer needed.

Julian didn't need to do a full inventory of the bins in that room to know there was enough there to keep the town through the winter months. He'd seen it before last winter, and the remnants of the winter stock in the previous spring when he and Readrick had first arrived in town.

He hadn't exactly been worried; hadn't thought about it at all during his journey in all honesty. But now seeing it, he felt a reassurance that he hadn't realized he needed. The town was well provisioned, one less danger of the winter avoided.

Raedrick pursed his lips as he scanned the storage room, then nodded. "Excellent. And yes, the mayor told me that as well." He looked away from the stored fish to Danil and made a little semi-apologetic grin at him, accompanied by a smidgen of a shrug. "Just feel better seeing it myself."

Danil nodded understanding. "And we've upgraded our security here after last spring's incident as well."

Horace snorted. "Not like anyone's going to steal from it."

"You never know," Danil replied, and Horace snorted again.

"Yes well," Raedrick said, "it doesn't hurt to be careful. One of us will stop by daily to check on things."

Danil looked like he wanted to object, but he merely nodded again. "As you wish, Constable."

7

LUNCHTALK

Julian considered as he stepped into The Oarlock that although he'd only been back in town for a day he was already becoming way too predictable. Coming here for dinner last night and now lunch today…

He snorted. Not like there was a better place for lunch in town. Holb didn't serve food, only ale. And sure there were other smaller kitchens around town that served comers, and he'd given them plenty of business over the months. But Molli made the best fish stew in the Vale, and anyway…

And anyway, as he doffed his cloak he admitted to himself that the place just felt like home. Almost as much as his flat did.

More so, actually, since his landlord had let his flat out to someone else while he was gone and he'd had to settle for different, smaller rooms, on the top floor. Smaller, and colder, then he'd had before.

Less rent. But still not what he had become accustomed to. And he wouldn't be able to truly look around for a better place until the spring thaw.

So Molli's inn was the next best thing to home; it certainly felt more familiar than any other place at the moment.

He hung his cloak from a hook by the door and moved toward the bar. Molli was there instead of Rolf, her grey hair up in a bun like normal and her white apron snugged tight over her dark blue dress as she filled a mug for one of the bar's patrons from the brass taps halfway down the wall behind the bar.

There were four men seated at the bar, two in a fishing man's grey cloak and two in the garments of tradesmen. Julian recognized both the fishing men, younger fellows who were still unwed, and one of the tradesmen. Tam, his name was, and he helped out at one of the canvas shops in town. The other fellow was new to his eye. More lightly complected than the fishing men, whose skin was tanned and weathered by hours out on the lake even now a couple weeks or more from their last expedition onto the water, with black hair that hung down to his shoulders. He had broad shoulders and looked to be well-muscled.

Julian found himself focusing in on the man as he drew nearer, wondering how he had not met the fellow before. But then Molli turned around and slid the mug across the bar to him, and when he went to take it, he moved enough in his seat so Julian could see the circled M stitched into the breast of the brown coat he was wearing.

The sign of Brice Melton's ranch. The fellow must be one of the hands working down there by the Hook.

They didn't come up to Lydelton all that often; no wonder Julian hadn't seen him before. Still, what could have brought him all the way up here in this weather?

Yes, it was sunny out. Today. But it was bloody cold and the wind was up, and it would take half a day to ride back down to the Melton ranch from here on the best of occasions. Must have some pressing business to attend to, or…

A woman's laugh, merry…almost girlish…drew his gaze away from the ranch hand, and Julian felt his eyebrows rising as he took in the sight in one of the booths over against the left wall.

Melanie was seated there, opposite the bard from the previous night. She had on her dark blue dress, with white lace at the hems and on the bodice, and had her dark brown hair held back from her face by a blue ribbon that matched her dress. The bard's coat was yellow this morning, a few shades lighter than his hair, which he let flow loosely about his shoulders.

The two of them had bowls—of fish stew no doubt—set before them, and the bard had a tankard. Melanie had a glass goblet filled with a deep red wine, and she was leaning back in her seat, amused delight written all over her face.

Their eyes met from across the room and Melanie's smile shifted slightly. She gestured for him to come closer. For a second he hesitated, curiosity over the Melton man's presence tugging at him. But only for a second. He wove his way past two empty tables and drew up next to the booth where she and the bard were seated, and saw the blond man looking at him curiously. His eyes flicked up and down Julian's body, and paused noticeably on his badge of office for a second.

"Julian," Melanie said, and scooted in on her booth seat to make some room. "Join us. You haven't met Hamel yet."

"Can't say I have, except for the performance last night," Julian said. He held out his hand to the bard. "Julian Hinderbrook."

The bard's hand was almost entirely devoid of calluses but his grip was firm. "A pleasure, Constable," he said.

"I would ask," Julian said as he slid into the spot on the bench that Melanie had vacated, "what brought you to our little town, but I heard you had some trouble with the weather."

Hamel made something between a wince and a smile, and nodded. "Yes. It seems the master of my caravan underestimated how quickly the seasons pass in these mountains. He seemed confident they could make it on to Calas, but the idea of tromping through weeks of snow was…unappealing. Especially compared with Lydelton's warm hospitality."

"Were you off to the front, then? We had some bards in my unit back when I was in the army. But I've heard the fighting's mostly over and treaty negotiations are in progress?"

Hamel shook his head. "I've no interest in military matters. No offense to those who do, but it's not for me." He looked away from Julian, toward the common room's front door. "Still, sometimes wanderlust takes hold, the urge to see new things." He looked a bit wistful for a second, then he looked back at Julian and made a little shrug. "You understand."

Julian nodded slowly. He did understand. "Well, if you've never experienced winter here, you haven't experienced it at all. Lots of fun things to do, actually."

Hamel's eyebrow quirked upward, his expression doubtful, and Melanie chuckled.

"You haven't seen comedy until you've seen Julian here on ice skates."

Julian gave her a sidelong look. She just looked back, a teasing smile ghosting across her lips, and he rolled his eyes.

"There's also ice fishing," he said, returning his attention to Hamel. "And some folks enjoy snowshoeing through the woods. And dog sledding."

"Really? I've heard of that, but never actually seen it. Does it hurt the dogs at all?"

Julian shook his head. "No, in fact they seem to like it. If you're interested, Povol is the man to see about that. He normally hangs out over at Holb's Tavern."

Hamel nodded. "I found that place a few days ago. Interesting setup, and I have to give credit to his customers's hardiness."

Holb's wasn't an indoor place like The Oarlock. He literally cut his bar into the side of a building and paved out a courtyard for his customers to enjoy their drink. For the winter months, he erected a canvas tent enclosing the courtyard, and set up braziers for heat. But drafts still blew through from time to time and it was never as comfortable as Molli's place.

It was also quite a bit more rough. But some people preferred that, and Holb did good business, even in the winter.

"Holb makes a good ale."

"You mean his wife does," Melanie put in, and Julian nodded, conceding the point.

"True. And I expect they'll appreciate a good performance over there as well."

Hamel chuckled. "Master Holb tried to make it look like he was putting up a fight, but we've made arrangements."

Julian grinned at him.

The soft swishing of skirts announced Tami's arrival, a tray holding a steaming bowl and a clay tankard balanced on her left hand as she stopped beside their booth.

"Hot from the pot, Constable," she said as she placed the bowl of stew carefully down in front of Julian.

He took a moment to inhale the vapors and sighed at the spices that sizzled the inside of his nose, causing his mouth to water immediately. "I thought after all this time away I would become mysterious again," Julian mused, then sighed. "But I guess not."

"Not when it comes to ordering lunch, anyway," Tami said with a chuckle. She set the tankard down in front of the bowl, then turned to make her way back toward the bar.

Julian watched her go for a second, and had to admire the way she still managed to be graceful even with her much-expanded belly. Then he looked away, back toward Melanie. "How's the undigging going?"

She shuddered slightly. "Mistress Tanly looked in on my place from time to time while I was away, but even still you would not believe the dust. And I think a family of mice took up residence at some point during the summer."

He winced. "That's going to be difficult to remedy."

"I can manage," she said, and arched an eyebrow at him.

"What was it that took you out of the vale?" Hamel said, his tone curious as he raised his tankard for a quick drink.

Julian took a spoonful of the stew and savored the rich flavor for a moment before swallowing. He washed it down with a swig of Molli's winter ale from the tankard Tami left before answering.

"A friend of ours had some business he needed help attending to."

Beside him, Melanie sipped at her goblet of wine, not speaking.

They had decided to keep the details of their journey discrete. Or as discrete as possible. The money they had brought back would send tongues to wagging, no doubt. But the rest... Probably best not to spread that word around beyond their little group.

Hamel clearly was curious to learn more, from the glimmer in his eye as he pondered Julian's words for a moment. But he merely said, "The business was successful, I hope?"

"Quite satisfactory," Melanie said, and drained the last of her wine with a longer sip. She set her goblet down on the table and pushed her bowl away, just a few chunks of fish and cut-up potatoes remaining in the bottom. Then she gave Julian a little nudge with her elbow.

"But if you'll excuse me, I'd best get back to getting my house in order."

Julian nodded and slid out of the booth, giving her room to get up.

She took a moment to smooth her dress while Julian took his seat back, then she inclined her head toward Hamel. "Pleasure meeting you, Master Hamel," she said with a friendly smile.

He inclined his head to her in a manner that made it almost appear a bow, though he didn't budge from his seat. "And you, Melanie."

She gave Julian's shoulder a little squeeze. "See you later?"

He nodded, and she meandered past the tables in the middle of the common room toward the door.

Julian noticed Hamel watching her go, a curious look on his face. After she donned her cloak and exited, the bard turned to look back at him, and something shifted in Hamel's expression.

"Fascinating woman. Are you and she...?" He gestured from Julian toward the door, which was closing behind her.

Julian blinked, unsure how to answer that question. He gave himself a second to think by taking another drink from his tankard. Finally, he decided on the truth.

"That is a long and complicated story."

"Ah." From the look on Hamel's face, Julian wasn't sure how he took that.

8

FRESH EYES

An afternoon spent criss-crossing town with Raedrick to check on the grocers and their supplies for the winter left the brief warmth of lunch in The Oarlock a longed-for memory. Despite the sky remaining clear, it felt like the air had gotten progressively colder as the afternoon wore on, and by the time they climbed up the trio of stairs leading to the porch fronting the Constabulary, Julian wished he had thought to put on another layer this morning.

The inside of their office was almost sweltering, it was such a contrast with the chill, and for a moment Julian stopped, slammed by the weight of it, just inside the door.

Raedrick closed the door behind them and shrugged off his cloak, then nodded to his right, toward the new desk. "I see you're back, Amos."

The man Julian had seen in The Oarlock earlier was seated there, scribbling onto a page of parchment with a quill pen. He had on the same brown coat with the circled M on its breast, but he had his hair tied back into a ponytail now. He shrugged in response to Raedrick's words and replaced his pen into its inkwell, then stood.

"There isn't much work left to be done this time of year on the ranch," he said. "We finished up the winter preps two days ago, and..." He shrugged again.

"And you couldn't stand the thought of languishing on the ranch for the rest of the winter, so you came back," Raedrick said.

Amos flushed, and nodded. Then his eyes flicked from Raedrick to Julian and he blinked, a question on his face.

Raedrick saw it as soon as Julian did, and chuckled. He gestured Julian's way. "Amos Melton, this is Julian Hinderbrook, my partner."

Amos blinked again. Twice. Then he flushed some more.

It was almost comic, but Julian decided to save him. "We haven't met before, but I saw you in The Oarlock earlier." He looked sidelong at Raedrick and grinned. "I thought he would be younger, from what you said before."

Amos flushed even more, and looked downward. "I...look older than I am," he said.

"You poor bastard," Julian said, shaking his head in mock pity. "When you're our age you'll be wishing the opposite." Then he stepped forward and extended his hand. "Nice to meet you."

Amos' grip was strong. No surprise from his muscular frame. But there was a hesitancy there despite the strength of his grip, and a naiveté in his eyes as they raised back up to meet Julian's as he shook.

That cast aside the illusion that his burly frame had formed, and in a flash Julian saw not a strong man but a lad still growing into himself, unsure of his place but wanting to find it. And hopeful that he could.

He liked the lad immediately.

"What are you working on?" Raedrick said as he took his seat behind his desk.

Amos shrugged and picked his parchment back up. He blew on it quickly, to help dry the ink, and held it out toward Julian. "Tallying up the payments you've made for prisoners's meals this year."

Julian blinked, and looked down at the parchment. It was

filled with notes of delivery and payment, with a running sum going down the right hand side of the page. He blinked again, then stepped over and handed the page to Raedrick.

"I never thought to do that before," he said, and Raedrick shook his head in agreement.

He perused the document, and his lips pursed. Just then the black goatee he wore didn't quite conceal the scar on his jaw; it seemed to pucker out from between the whiskers like it was trying to escape.

"I didn't realize we spent so much." He looked back over at Amos, an eyebrow lifting.

The young man shrugged. "I found the invoices tucked into your files." He gestured toward the book case adjacent to the cell block door. "It looked like no one had done anything with them, so…" He shrugged again.

"Well the prisoners have to eat," Julian said.

Amos nodded. "But catered meals from The Oarlock? There are cheaper ways to spend the town's money."

On the one hand, Julian knew Amos was probably right. He and Raedrick hadn't really considered it before. It just seemed natural to utilize Molli's kitchen, since she had the facilities and did a good job of it. And…

He looked at Raedrick and it was obvious he was thinking the same thing he was.

They had just defaulted to using Molli because they knew and liked her, and Raedrick was sweet on Lani, and… And well, that wasn't really fair to the other people in town at all, was it?

"The mayor never had an issue with our budget and how we spent it," he said, and he could hear in his own voice that he was trying to justify their lack of consideration.

"But he didn't look at it very closely either, and we never really thought about it before," Raedrick said, and he frowned deeply. He sighed and scanned over the page again, then looked back over at Amos. "This isn't complete."

Amos shook his head. "I've only gotten through the first quarter of the year."

"Well finish, and then look back over the three previous years, to how Constable Malory handled this sort of thing."

"Then I guess you can start looking at alternatives," Julian said.

Amos nodded immediately. He looked positively eager to be about it.

Julian moved over to his desk and lowered himself into the chair. "On the bright side, we're releasing Trevir tomorrow, right?"

Raedrick nodded.

"Well hopefully we'll have plenty of time before we need to buy prisoner meals again."

The look Raedrick gave him conveyed entire worlds of doubt.

9

WINTER'S FOLLY

olb's Tavern somehow seemed warmer than the common room of The Oarlock had been at lunch time, despite night having fully fallen by the time Julian stepped through the flap of the canvas siding that separated the tavern's seating area from the steadily-decreasing temperature of the world outside.

The warmth struck him like a hammer, and he felt the urge to shrug off his cloak and bask in it. Then a light gust from the still-open flap behind him drove that thought away, and he closed the flap in a rush.

Holb's was much as Julian remembered it, except that there were two more tables for four than before, and three more braziers. A full dozen of the fire stands were now set up at the periphery of the tent, lending light and warmth to the entirety. Combined with a crowd that filled every seat and left a dozen or so men to stand adjacent to the cut-out bar, it was no wonder the place was so warm.

Julian whistled softly and weaved his way past a couple tables, meandering toward the bar. He couldn't remember ever seeing the place this full. Not that Holb ever lacked for customers, but he never got the crowds Molli did. Partly on account of the outdoor nature of his setup and partly on account of Holb himself.

The man was holding court behind the bar, tall and burly and bald with a thick brown beard that came halfway down his neck and compressed lips that seemed almost on the edge of a snarl. His muscles strained the sleeves of the deep blue tunic he wore so that Julian could practically hear the seams screaming for mercy as he moved his arm to wipe down the bartop in front of himself with a white rag.

As Julian stepped up, Holb's left eyebrow twitched, and he gave the smallest of nods in greeting. "Constable."

"Good to see you, Holb. You've made some changes, I see. Looks good." Julian rubbed at his chin and grinned, but Holb just looked at him. Apparently he didn't care for the compliment on his beard. "Got any of your amber?"

Holb shook his head. "That's gone with the summer." He turned toward one of the two kegs that he had stacked behind the bar and snatched a tankard from a shelf nearby. A moment later, he turned back to Julian and plunked the tankard down.

White foam rose to just above the rim of the tankard and as Julian leaned his head to look at it, he smelled hops and something else…was that lemon?

He looked back up at Holb and raised a questioning eyebrow.

Holb shrugged, and gestured toward the tankard.

Julian hefted the tankard and took a swig, and stopped mid-swallow as the multi-layered flavors of the brew settled onto his tongue. Yes, that was lemon, or something like it. With hops floating overtop. But what was the rest… He couldn't name them, but they all cascaded together into a whole that was delicious.

And judging from the immediate rush of heat that came after he swallowed it down, potent.

"Good stuff," he said, lifting the tankard toward Holb in salute. "What do you call it?"

"Winter's Folly."

Julian nodded. He fished a couple coins from his pouch and

set them onto the bar as payment. Then he turned around to look at the rest of the tented area more fully, and he noticed the small stage that had been set up at the far end, directly across a gap between the rows of tables from the bar.

"Hamel told me he'd be playing here from time to time," he said, nodding toward the stage. "I guess that accounts for the crowd?"

Holb grunted.

"What kind of deal did you two work out for that?"

"His business. And mine."

But not yours, the tavern keeper didn't say. And Julian decided not to press the issue. It didn't really matter.

All the same as he looked around at the throng, greater than any he had ever seen here, he couldn't help feeling part of the same unease he'd felt the previous night during Hamel's performance after Raedrick and Lani left.

Good music was one thing, and the gods new there was little enough new entertainment in the Vale once the winter set in and caravans stopped coming. But still...

He thought back to the way the bard's music had seemed to grab him and carry him away before, and how the crowd at The Oarlock had looked with such hostility toward Raedrick and Lani for a moment...

The flap he had just come through opened, and two figures came in. The first was Melanie, dressed in a midnight-blue dress with silver lace at the bodice and a silver belt around her waist, and a matching cloak about her shoulders. Her cowl was thrown back, and her flowing brown curls were hanging freely down to just past her shoulders. She was flush from the cold outside, her cheeks rosy, and she had a smile of enjoyment on her face as she said something to the person who came in behind her.

The room stilled as her companion straightened from tying the flap closed and his cowl fell back. It was Hamel, his hair pulled back into a ponytail this evening. His cloak was grey-blue, and he wore his harp case on his back just like the previous evening. And he was grinning in response to whatever Melanie had said.

He opened his mouth to reply, but clapping from half of the tables in the tent, sporadic at first and then coalescing quickly into a sustained applause of greeting stopped whatever it was he was going to say.

He blinked, then seemed to take a second to gather himself. And it was like he grew three inches. His back went spear-shaft straight and he smiled broadly at the crowd, then lifted his hand in a wave of greeting as his eyes swept across the people waiting for him.

Because of course they were. Holb sold great beer, but there were people amongst the crowd at the tables that Julian knew for a fact hadn't set foot here in the last year and a half, at least. Julian even saw ex-Mayor Brimly at a table at the far end of the tent, and he and Holb decidedly did not get along.

The clapping died down after a few seconds, and Hamel made a half-bow. When he rose his smile was, if anything, even wider than before.

"Thank you, my friends," he said, in a voice that easily carried throughout the tent. "You are too kind."

He turned away from Melanie and moved toward the waiting stage, and for a second she got an almost sour expression on her face. Then it faded and she turned toward the bar. Her eyes swept over the room and alighted on Julian, and the smile returned. She threaded her way past the same tables he had and a moment later was at his side.

"I see you and Holb are becoming re-acquainted," she said, gesturing toward his tankard.

Julian held it out to her. "It's his new one. Pretty good, actually."

Melanie wrinkled her nose and shook her head. "No. Thank you."

"Your loss." He took a slow draw and savored the flavors for a moment, then swallowed. "I don't think I've ever seen you in here before."

She looked around at the inside of the tent, then glanced at Holb behind the bar. "Yes, I prefer places that are a bit less rough around the edges. Or at least ones that serve wine."

Not exactly a shocking revelation. Julian chuckled.

She looked at him sidelong for a moment as though to discern the source of his amusement, and he just grinned at her.

"Anyway, I see I'm not the only new face. Is that Mayor Brimly? I can't imagine him being a regular."

Julian shook his head. "He isn't. But it seems Hamel draws a crowd." He nodded toward where Hamel had set his harp case down and was getting situated.

"As well he should. Musicians of his quality are rare to find even in large cities, let alone a—"

"A flyspeck of a town in the middle of nowhere, inhabited by bumpkins?" Julian said, recalling how she had referred to Lydelton when they first met.

Melanie looked him askance, then shrugged, a wry half-grin appearing on her face for a moment. "I expect the crowds will dwindle after a week or two, when his presence is less of a novelty."

Julian took another swig from his tankard, and it seemed like the warmth from his belly as it went down flashed a bit hotter this time. "What did he have to say as you two walked over?"

She arched an eyebrow at him. "We didn't walk over. I bumped into him right outside." He felt the pressure of her gaze and turned his head to look at her more fully, and the other eyebrow rose to join the first. That half-grin appeared again, this time more teasing.

"Why Julian, you aren't jealous, are you?"

Julian snorted. "Not sure I trust him. Whatever you said before, I'm still not comfortable about what happened last night."

She rolled her eyes and looked back across the room to where Hamel was now up on his seat, tuning his harp.

The tent was quiet, far more quiet than Julian could recall from his previous times in Holb's last winter. And all but a few eyes were fixed on the bard as he finished his preparations. The pair of servings girls in Holb's employ still made their rounds to the various tables, though they were moving a bit more slowly than normal, and they often shifted to look over at Hamel as well.

Probably Melanie was right. It was just the novelty of having a real, no kidding bard in a town where the best music normally available came from the throats and strings of the few locals who had the time to practice with anything approaching regularity.

And some of them were pretty good. But not compared with what Julian had seen from Hamel last night.

It was just excitement, and appreciation for obvious talent. That was...

Hamel began to play, and almost at once Julian found his thoughts drawn down beneath the melody that the bard's fingers evoked from his instrument.

It was different from the night before. More haunting, almost unearthly, like the essence of something lurking just unseen but still imminent, ready to make an appearance.

A shiver went up Julian's spine, and he flashed back to the Out-Dweller that the mad mage Terulian had brought to town a year and a half ago. But then the chords shifted, and the unearthly feeling shifted to something less sinister. Like the thing that was lurking just out of sight was merely watching, or maybe wanting to help.

Then Hamel's voice joined his fingers on the strings, and the dual nature of the chord progression solidified. He sang of powers great, some good and some evil, dueling over the destinies of a group of mortals who, unbeknownst to them, had their fates hanging on the outcome of the duel.

On the song flowed, the battle ebbing and flowing from one side to the other, and each time it shifted Julian felt something within himself lurch, like it wasn't the made-up people in Hamel's song that hang in the balance but himself. Himself and everyone he held dear.

He could almost see them, the titanic forces engaged in battle. Slavering fangs dripping onto the ground, where the earth hissed away into oblivion at the spittle's touch. Great claws flailing about, seeking to rend and tear, and he saw them, the entity's intended victims.

Faces swam before Julian's eyes. Raedrick and Lani. Little Celia. His parents and his brother. Horace. Gilroy and Hiram. The faces of his squad-mates from back in the army—somewhere in the back of his mind something screamed that they were all dead, all but Jared, but he barely heard it. And last of all…

Her face twisted into a scream of agony as the claws rent her. The dark curls of her hair shifted to red as her blood flowed, and Julian felt a growl rumble up from the depths of his belly. He stepped forward, intent on revenge. On justice, and—

"Julian!"

A hand gripped his upper arm, hard, and the world congealed back to reality.

He was in Holb's tent, and all eyes were on him. Across the tent, on his stool, Hamel was staring at him without expression, but the man's eyes seemed to burrow into Julian's soul.

He shook himself and forced his eyes away and down to the hand on his arm, then up its own arm.

And there she was, not torn asunder by those horrible claws, but whole and well. His heart wanted to leap for joy, but the expression on her face…

Confusion, concern, but above all, fear almost rising to panic.

And he realized what else the arm she was gripping had done. The tankard was gone, lying at his feet and the ale it had contained was spreading out in an expanding pool on the paving stones. But more that that, he had drawn his sword halfway from its scabbard. Even now, the light from the dozen braziers standing around the tent made the clean blade shine with a red-orange light, as though it hungered, yearned for the blood he was about to feed it.

Blood? Whose blood? What—

"Get out."

That was Holb's voice, and when Julian looked back at him, the burly bartender was staring at him with eyes that would fell a deer at a hundred paces.

"I..." He stammered, unsure what to say or how to say it, and Melanie's hand tightened on his arm.

The song still soared in his ears, and for a second he felt the urge to surge froward, to lay waste...to who?

Julian snarled, and tried again to speak, but the only thing that came out was a croak.

He paused for a second, and the urge to charge remained.

Instead, he released the grip of his sword. It slid home into its scabbard with a clack that he didn't register. The only sound that reached his ears, beneath the chords that still swam in his brain, was the howl of the wind as he fled through the tent flap and out into the night.

But he felt the eyes of the bard on his back the whole way out.

Melanie watched Julian storm from the tent, dumbstruck.

Her mind was awhirl as she raced back over the events of the last several minutes. One minute everything had been normal. She had been humming along to the melody Hamel had been playing, and felt herself swept along in the drama that his lyrics were unfurling. As she listened, memories floated forth from deep within, memories she hadn't dwelt on in years, the hurt was too deep.

She recalled the twin spires of the Morested Academy's central building, seeming to poke into the sky like spear tips beneath a waning crescent moon as she and Timon entered the grounds for a performance. The smell of him, masculine but also gentle, and the feel his strong arm where her hand laid in the crook of his elbow.

The enchanting melodies as the orchestra put on its show, taking her to heights of musical experience she had never considered before.

Here, on his own, Hamel couldn't dream to recreate that effect, but he was doing a stellar job nonetheless, just as he had the previous night. And Melanie was enjoying it completely…

Until Julian's snarl, nigh-on a shout of rage, rang out from next to her, and he moved to spring forward. His hand was on his sword, and he had his eyes locked on Hamel from across the room. What was he doing?

She reached out to grab his arm as all eyes turned onto them…

The tent flap fell shut behind him and silence loomed for a second. Then Hamel cleared his throat and said something. It was in a light-hearted tone, but it evoked chuckles, half-hearted at first but then more genuine after a moment, from the entire crowd. And it seemed the tension was leaving as quickly as it had sprung up.

But Melanie didn't hear. Not fully. She was up and halfway toward the tent flap before she realized she was moving.

"Let him go," someone said nearby, but she brushed the words off and followed Julian outside.

The darkness was deep, compared with the light inside Holb's tent. The sudden cold pummeling.

But the dark wasn't complete, and she could see Julian's form stalking away by the light spilling from windows on either side of the street, moving to the east toward his flat. Or The Oarlock.

"Julian, wait!" she said, and hurried to catch up to him.

He was moving quickly, but she caught up after half a block, and reached out to touch his shoulder. "Julian!"

At her touch, he whirled, his eyes alight, and for a second it looked like he was about to reach for his sword again. But just as quickly as that impression came, it fled. He recognized her, and his eyes narrowed. She saw confusion and more in his eyes.

"You felt it, didn't you?"

Melanie shook her head. "Felt what?"

Julian scowled and pointed back behind her toward Holb's. "What he did! I don't care what you say, Melanie. That wasn't normal!"

His face, normally so pleasant—more than pleasant—to look at, was tight, lines standing out around his mouth and eyes from the tension in his facial muscles. His eyes were narrowed, looking past her now back toward the tent like he was trying to see through some puzzle toward its solution.

What was he talking about?

"Julian, he was playing and singing. Well, I'll grant you, but that was all."

A loud snort, almost as loud as the snarl-shout he'd made inside, preceded a violent shake of his head.

"If anyone did anything, it was you. What were you getting at?"

Julian recoiled, his eyes returning to focus in on her, and she saw something in them…something almost dark. A shiver went up her spine, and she had to restrain herself from backing away from him.

But no, she could never believe he could mean her harm.

For an instant, though…

The whatever-it-was in his eyes lessened, and that feeling of danger passed. His expression turned confused, quizzical. He shook his head again and spread his hands, helplessly.

"I don't know." He drew a deep breath. "It was like…" He inhaled deeply and threw his head back, looking up into the clouded-over darkness of the night sigh in exasperation. "I don't know!"

"Ok," she said, slowly. "It's ok, Julian."

"No it isn't!" His attention back toward the tavern over her shoulder. "That guy is up to something, I'm telling you."

Impossible for him to cause her harm or no, he was behaving erratically. Melanie couldn't ever recall seeing him in this sort of state before. That shiver of nerves came back, but she forced them down.

"It's been a hard few weeks," she said, "and we're all tired."

Julian let out a bitter-sounding half-laugh. "You think I'm losing it, don't you? Over needing a nap?"

"No. But you *are* tired. I know I have been."

He looked at her in silence for a long moment, then he shrugged and turned away, back in the direction he had been walking when she caught up to him. "Maybe you're right," he said, but he didn't sound like he believed it.

Melanie watched him walk away, and for a moment she considered that she should follow, make certain he got home alright.

Silly woman, he's a grown man. What are you going to do, tuck him into bed?

That thought brought a rush of conflicting feelings through her, embarrassment and intrigue both at the notion. But she pressed that aside. Mostly. The state he was in, he might not welcome the help home, either way.

And besides…

She turned to look back at tent enclosing Holb's tavern, a bit of dark slightly lighter than the other shadows in the distance, and decided that she didn't need to ruin her evening just because Julian had gone off on a flight of fancy.

So instead of following him, she made her way back to the tent, and the performance.

UNREQUITED RAGE

The scene in Holb's had settled back to normal when Melanie slipped back inside the canvas flap and into the light and warmth within. Hamel was still on his stool off to the right, plucking out a melody on his harp that immediately made her think of a gentle brook descending through a mountain meadow, the warmth of summer being set off by a breeze that carried the scent of moisture and the chirping of songbirds.

A calm, gentle melody, simple but relaxing that seemed to take whatever anxiety she still held over Julian's outburst and cast it aside.

Some of the patrons had shifted. More men were standing around the bar, leaving chairs open in the tables arrayed before Hamel, and Melanie made her way toward the closest empty one and sat down.

The fellow next to her was a man she recognized by face—hard to find someone in Lydelton she hadn't seen before—but not by name. He had a decade or more on her and was dressed in well broken-in leathers and furs sewed together. One of the local mountaineers, from the look of him. He was cradling a tankard in both hands and listening to the music with a small half-smile on his black-bearded face.

When she sat, he glanced at her, then did a double-take and smiled broadly in greeting. His teeth were yellowing and he was missing the left front one on the top of his mouth, leaving a wide gap in his smile. Somehow that gave his face a bit of charm that the lines on his forehead and around his eyes would have denied.

"Nice to see you, Mistress Klemins," he said, and she nodded in reply.

"Good evening."

"What's got the Constable so worked up?" The mountaineer leaned a bit closer, and she could smell the ale on his breath. The same stuff Julian had been drinking.

Melanie shook her head. "Stress from a long journey. He'll be fine in the morning."

The mountaineer grunted and took a drink from his tankard.

On the stool, Hamel brought the tune to a conclusion with a slow, almost luxurious arpeggio. Silence lingered for a second and then the patrons clapped, almost in unison. Less boisterous applause than the people in The Oarlock had given him last night, but then it was a less energetic tune.

Hamel made a sort of seated half-bow at the applause. As he raised his head back up, his eyes swept the room, and it seemed to Melanie they lingered on her for a moment before moving on. But then, she could see the other patrons perking up a bit as his attention swept over them.

Good showmanship.

"This next one is old, going back to the founding of the Kingdom," he said. "Not many even know how to play it these days." His eyebrows waggled, and he got a twinkle in his eye as he added, "So you should feel blessed." Then he chuckled, and several others in the crowd responded in kind.

A single chord, strummed languidly but with precision, swept all sound from the room except for his, and Hamel began.

The notes rang somewhat discordant at first, like the song didn't know what it wanted to be. But slowly, almost imperceptibly, it shifted, the dissonant notes fading one by one into the melody until, after a few moments, Melanie couldn't even recall what had been so jarring about its opening at all.

It was beautiful. Beautiful, and sad, haunting even.

Hamel's singing told a story of unrequited love, love so strong it drew near to obsession. But of course the object of that love was married to another, and the songwriter mourned and lamented for what could never be.

The song shifted then. The beauty remained, but now the chord progression was dark, no longer sad but brooding, morose and bitter as love grew into obsession and past, becoming jealousy that festered into anger. Murderous anger.

Melanie could feel the mountaineer shifting in his seat, see the scowl forming on his lips even as she felt her own heart twisted about.

The poor woman that Hamel sang of. Target of such obsession, such rage. Could she not see what it was building toward, or was he the kind that hid his feelings and intentions beneath a facade of friendship?

More likely the latter. She had known a few low men like that; what woman had not? Fortunately she had been able to smell them out before they could do any harm, but she knew of other women who had not. Had not seen the danger the obsessed man presented before—

Hamel's voice shifted, the lyrics coming out in a near growl as the song took an even darker turn. The anger boiled over, the rage turned the songwriter's vision red, and he set out to exact his revenge on the man who had stolen his love from him.

And on her, for never recognizing what she should have seen right in front of her, in him.

The attack came as a complete surprise. The raging man struck from behind, cracking the top of his head, and he fell without even a scream. She stared in shock for a moment at the sight of her love, destroyed so, at the feet of the man she had once thought a friend.

His chest heaved with frightful energy, and when she raised

her eyes back to his face she only saw murder in those eyes. Those hazel eyes beneath close-cropped brown hair.

He started toward her, fists wrapped around the cudgel he had used to kill her husband, and she screamed then. Screamed, and turned to run.

But she didn't know this part of the city, and which way to turn to find help. The streets were deserted; why was there no one around?

He was hot on her heels; she could practically feel the fire of his breathing as he gave chase.

Panic welled up within her and she darted down a narrow alley between two buildings that only registered as shadows in the reddish light that seemed to follow her as she went.

Light caused by the depth of his rage?

It didn't make any sense, she only knew she had to run, had to get away.

The alley bent to the left.

And ended in a brick wall half a dozen paces later.

Brick? Hadn't the buildings been wooden?

"Now you're mine," she heard, but it wasn't spoken aloud, more like she could hear her attacker's thoughts, feel the insane, murderous glee as his final victory over fate's injustice finally drew near.

She turned to face him, back pressed up against the wall, desperately wanting to sink into it, to get away.

In the back of her mind, something stirred, some knowledge that she knew she should be able to take hold of, that she could use to ward him off.

But whatever it was, it would not come, and all she could see as he raised the cudgel with both hands over his head was the burning in his eyes, the lust twisted to raging hatred mixed with the ecstasy of madness.

Then the club came down. She wanted to cringe away, but his stare held her eyes fast.

Whistling through the air as the club descended…

And a final chord rang out, discordant so as to make the beginning of the song seem like the most well-crafted melody ever composed, and the interior of Holb's Tavern sprang back into reality all around her.

She realized she had drawn back in her seat, cringing into it like she had been against the wall. Her hands were clenched into fists and she felt pain in her palms.

She looked down, and forced her fingers open, then gasped as she saw blood where her nails had dug in. She felt the yelp she let out more than heard herself make it.

The mountaineer looked her askance, then his expression turned to one of concern as he took a good look at her.

"Mistress Klemins? Are you alright?"

She was trembling, and her palms were wet, a mixture of sweat and blood. All she could do was shake her head and mumble something, she did not know what.

Hamel had stood and was making a bow to applause that was loud but also uncertain, like the crowd didn't quite know what to make of the song. He said something about needing to take a break, to wet his throat before he could sing some more.

Someone back by the bar said they had his drink covered, and he nodded with a smile. He took a moment to set his harp down by the stool, then he swept between the tables to accept the proffered drink.

Melanie just watched him, unable to fully process what she had just experienced.

As he passed her table, she thought his eyes flicked toward her for a moment, and his lips twitched.

"Mistress Klemins?" the mountaineer said again, and she shook her head.

"I... I need to go home," she said, and heard her voice trembling.

Then she stood. And fled.

12

MORNING READING

Strange dreams kept Melanie tossing and turning most of the night, so when dawn's light finally brightened her eastern windows, she rose feeling gravelly-eyed, with a dry mouth and almost as fatigued as when she first laid down.

All the same, she forced herself from her bed and went about her morning routine. She picked out a dark grey dress with silvery-white lace at the bodice and a sash to match, which she tightened about her waist with a double-bowed knot. Then she set about getting her hair done just right, so it didn't look like a mass of tangles. A plain silver necklace that fit tight against her neck completed her ensemble, and she tucked her pouch of pre-made components that she always kept on her person behind the sash. Then she headed down from her upstairs rooms to the main floor of her little house, where her shop, Melanie's Mystical Crafts, lay.

She had spent most of the last day dusting and cleaning upstairs, and it was just about fit to live in again. Though she might have to borrow a cat from someone to help with the mice.

Downstairs, though…

She looked at the racks of trinkets and charms that dominated the center of the front room, and the shelves against the wall opposite the door, and frowned at the work that still needed doing. She almost considered ignoring it, and going to The Oarlock for breakfast instead. But she'd wasted too much time there yesterday, and besides…

Besides, Hamel might be there. And after last night's events…

She still felt unsettled, and her dreams hadn't helped. Before that last song, she thought Julian was overreacting. But now, now she was not so sure. There was something about that experience that resonated through her mind. Something she'd read, or heard of. Maybe back in the Capital with Timon?

She needed to figure it out.

Behind the counter that she'd put in place at the rear of her shop was a curtained-off doorway to her storage room and a small kitchen. Her little wood-fired stove stood in the corner next to a stack of tinder and a larger stack of fuel. A glance within said that whatever coals still had any heat to them would be insufficient to light even the most dry tinder, so instead she just tossed some of the larger fuel logs inside, then pulled a small, rolled-up wad of paper tied with a red thread from her components pouch.

A brief incantation later, the paper and its contents puffed away into oblivion, consumed to lend energy to her spell, and flames began licking upward from the fuel she'd just put into place.

Nodding in satisfaction, she stuck a piece of tinder into the stove to light it, then used it to light a candle that she had left on the kitchen's work counter. She closed the door of the stove and put a tea kettle on to boil, then she picked up the candle and went back into her storage room.

It took up half of the first floor's area, but it was quite a bit smaller than she would have preferred. Though in truth, she really didn't need much more space than she had, considering the small customer base that Lydelton provided. Still, as she looked upon the lone bookshelf along the rear wall, and the fact that it was already just about filled with the books she'd had delivered from her contacts in Mangin City, she yearned for more.

Enough of that.

She paused to set alight a candelabra that was mounted on the wall adjacent to the doorway, then she wove her way past a pair of chests and another shelf stacked with boxes that contained her inventory of components and other items for trade, and stood in front of the bookshelf.

The odor of old leather and aging pages filtered in above that of the candle smoke as she began scanning the collection of tomes.

Now where was that…?

By the time she found the book she was looking for and returned to her little kitchen, the tea kettle was whistling. She took a moment to pour a mug and grab a hunk of cheese from her cupboard, then she went back out to her shop, settled onto the stool behind her counter, and opened the book.

Time passed almost without her noticing the growing light from outside as the sun rose higher, so deeply was she into her search. She flipped page after page, sometimes skimming, sometimes reading deeply, but the answer she sought eluded her.

It was there, somewhere, but…where?

She gave a start when she raised her mug to her lips and found it empty. Blinking, she looked down and realized the cheese was all gone as well.

Then the little bell above her door rang out.

It gave her a little shock of surprise, and she snapped back up in time to see Raedrick walk into her shop.

He was wearing the cloak and broach she had made him as a wedding present, and below that tight black leggings tucked into calf-high boots and a grey-blue coat. His sword was on his hip and, as always, his hair was tied back in a ponytail. From the slightly reddish-tint to the cloaks's fabric, she saw that the dweomer she had embedded in the broach was active.

And no wonder. Despite the brightness of the day outside, as he stepped in a chilly breeze came with him that momentarily dispelled the warmth that her stove had brought to the shop.

"Close the door, please," she said, and he chuckled, but took a moment to pull it to with a solid thump.

"Good morning, Melanie," he said, and stepped over to the counter in front of her.

"I was just about to pour myself another mug of tea. Would you like one?"

"Please. It's a cold one today."

She snorted and said, "It's the warmest its going to be for months to come," then went back to her tea kettle.

Raedrick was silent when she placed a steaming mug down in front of him, and she cocked an eyebrow his way.

"So, to what do I owe this pleasure?"

Raedrick's lips turned downward into a frown for a heartbeat, but he didn't say anything at first. He picked up his mug and inhaled the rising vapors from it. His eyes widened slightly and he nodded approvingly before taking a long drink.

When he finally lowered the mug, his expression was serious. Not stern exactly, but something between concerned and troubled. "I heard about what happened last night in Holb's."

No surprise there. Melanie nodded.

"I'm concerned."

Melanie nodded again. "I don't think you need to be. Julian can be emotional at times, but—"

"About both of you."

That stopped Melanie in her tracks. She looked at him, and saw that he was deadly serious.

"People are saying you freaked out a bit as well. Almost as much as Julian did." He paused. "Except for the drawing steel part."

Melanie mulled it over. Had she? Had she really? She had reacted strongly, that was certain. But with what she had experienced, could anyone blame her? They all must have had a similar reaction to the—

A shiver went up her spine, not from the lingering chill of the room that the stove had not completely dispelled. But from where her own thoughts were leading her. Had been leading her ever since she departed the tavern last night.

She set her cup down and tapped the book that still lay open on the countertop. "I'm beginning to think Julian may have been right."

Raedrick cocked his head to the side slightly. "About Hamel?"

She shook her head. "Maybe? I'm not sure. But after last night…" She went on to describe what she had experienced, and Raedrick's lips turned more downward the longer she talked. Finally, she finished, and patted the book again.

"Something about it triggered a memory. Something I'd read or seen somewhere. That's what I've been doing this morning, trying to find it."

"So you think Hamel is, what, some kind of mage?"

"No. If he was using magic of that sort, it would be obvious to a trained observer."

"What do you mean, of that sort?"

Melanie cocked an eyebrow at him. "Come now, Raedrick. You surely must know the Magestirium is not the sole source of mystical power in the universe. Do you think that Out-Dweller we fought used the same sort of spells that they do, or I?"

"Well, no. But that thing wasn't human. And the Kingdom's laws regarding magic forbid anyone but the Magestirium from practicing it."

"And clearly that stops everyone from doing so," she said, putting an ironic lilt into her tone. After all, she was not part of the Magestirium. Could not be, as a woman. And yet she was a practitioner nonetheless.

By special dispensation, granted. But still…

Raedrick looked her askance for a second, then chuckled and nodded, conceding the point.

"It may be that Hamel found another source of power, one that we haven't encountered before." She paused. "Or it may just be that Julian and I were more tired from our journey than either of us thought, and a few days recovery will set everything right. That's what I am working to figure out."

Raedrick nodded slowly, and drank from his tea again. "Well, let me know what you find out. But I have to tell you, I'm dubious. Hamel's been in town for two weeks, and there haven't been any issues. He's been a stand-up citizen the entire time. The whole town loves him. Then you two come back and start in on him?" He set the cup down. "Doesn't sit well."

Melanie blinked.

Surely Raedrick must be joking…but the expression on his face was grimly serious, his eyes sharp, almost accusing.

"No one is starting in on him, Raedrick. What are you on about?"

Silence for a long moment, then Raedrick sniffed and waved a dismissive hand. A ghost of a smile flitted across his lips as he said, "You know what I mean. He's become pretty popular, is all."

Melanie nodded slowly, chewing on his words for a moment. The oddness of them rang through her brain like a gong, and she felt a little shiver run down her spine

"I'll keep that in mind," she said finally, and Raedrick nodded.

He did smile then, more genuinely, and gestured toward her book. "I'll let you get back to your mystery then."

The bell over the door tinkled as he stepped out, seeming to ring in the air for far longer than it should have.

Melanie just stared at the closed door, feeling that shiver again. After some uncounted time, the bell's ringing stopped, and the quiet jerked Melanie back to the present. With a deep frown, she looked back at her book.

The answer was there, somewhere. She thought. She hoped.

With a renewed feeling of urgency, prompted by unease, she dove back into the text.

❧ 13 ❧

PALAVER

The fish warehouse somehow seemed to stink even worse than it had yesterday. Julian would have thought that impossible, considering the icy conditions in the winter storeroom. The fish were solidly packed within layers of ice, and now snow, and thoroughly frozen. He assumed.

So how could it smell so much worse?

He grimaced and shook his head, forcing himself to not cover his nose as he walked with Horace past the last of the storage bins. Instead he focused his attention on the condition of the storeroom, looking for signs someone had compromised its security at all.

Of course there weren't any.

He picked up the pace a bit.

Beside him, Horace raised an eyebrow, and his lips twisted into an amused half-grin.

Julian saw it but chose not to respond. He just got the far end of the storeroom and finished his inspection, then nodded. "Looks all secure."

"You almost sound surprised," Horace said, then that look of amusement returned. "Or is your stomach just giving you problems?"

Julian raised an eyebrow at him, and Horace looked, if anything, even more amused.

"Heard you tied it on pretty well last night," he said. "Delicate stomachs tend to follow from that."

Julian snorted, and Horace chuckled, then clapped him on the shoulder. "Come on. Let's get in where it's warm."

The front room of the warehouse wasn't much warmer at all, though it was a bit, but in the Covington Brothers's office at the end of the space there was a wood stove, and as Julian followed Horace inside it felt like stepping into an oven, the contrast was so severe.

He stopped to close the door behind himself and took a moment to look around. Since the incident where the business had been robbed, Julian had only been back in here once, maybe twice. It hadn't changed all that much, except that the brothers had replaced their old, destroyed safe with one half again as large and much more robustly constructed.

Despite that, he felt an almost resonance in the place for a second. He flashed back to that morning when Danil had led he and Raedrick into this room, and they saw Jakob still bleeding from the attack that accompanied the robbery. And for a second, Julian had the idea that if he looked away from the safe he would see Jakob still sitting there, stunned and bleeding.

Silly, of course. But the feeling was there, nonetheless.

He shivered, and noticed Horace looking at him oddly.

"What?"

Horace shrugged—more like rolled his shoulders—and settled down into the swivel chair behind the desk.

"You tell me."

Julian frowned. "I wasn't drunk last night."

Horace grunted. "Easier to understand if you were. So what's the story? Half the town is talking about it this morning."

"Yeah," Julian looked away from him toward the room's one window. It was frosted over on the outside. "I've been wondering that myself. It's hard to explain."

He tried, though. Talking slowly, he recited to Horace what had happened, what he had experienced, at Holb's. When he finished, he looked back at the old man and spread his hands. "Maybe I'm just going crazy."

Horace grunted. "That boat sailed a long time ago," he said, with a teasing twinkle in his eyes.

Julian chuckled, though he didn't feel particularly mirthful. "That's what Melanie said, too."

Horace raised an eyebrow, and Julian shrugged.

"Well, not in those words. She said I was just tired, and overre-acting to good music."

Horace grunted. "She's not wrong very often, you know." He leaned forward in his chair slightly. "You all had a long journey, and you jumped right back into things as soon as you got back."

"And what, I'm just letting it get to me because I'm tired?"

Horace shrugged again, but the look on his face said it all: yes, yes you are.

Julian threw up his hands. "I wish I could believe that. But there's something more going on here, I'm sure of it."

"Well," the old man said, "what are you going to do about it?"

Julian just looked at him for a bit, his thoughts spinning. What *could* he do about it? And what if there was no "it" to do about, after all? Horace was right, he maybe should have taken a couple days to get re-settled before he got back about his duties as constable.

Hell, he'd barely fully unpacked from his journey and gotten himself settled into his new flat. Even the sack carrying his take of Feirhard's treasure was just tucked under the mattress of his bed, not someplace secure.

And why the hell hadn't he taken the time to do that, at least?

He needed to get a strongbox, and secure the box in place, then get the rest of his stuff squared away before he went off on wild investigations.

And investigations into what? What was he going to do, follow Hamel around town and spy out his every movement—

His mind snapped to, and Julian felt himself straighten, unconsciously. "Nothing, I guess. I don't trust that guy, though."

Horace nodded slowly. "Well, I've only seen him play a couple times. He cuts a nice tune. But I gotta say, most of the folks around town like him a lot. All sorts have been talking about how great it would be if he stayed here after the snows melt."

"So?"

"So, tread carefully. People won't react well if you start defaming their new favorite neighbor."

Defaming?

Julian narrowed his eyes, and studied Horace's face for a second. He looked his normal, grumpy but good-natured, self. But there was something in that tone, and there was a shadow in his eyes just then.

Julian got a little shiver down his spine.

"I'm not looking to do that," he said. Then he grinned. "But you're right. I'm probably just overreacting." He paused, then decided to change the subject. "Do you know if Jamie the carpenter is still open for business?"

Horace blinked, looking almost flustered for a second, then he nodded. "No reason he wouldn't be."

"Good. I need to see him about some furniture for my new place."

Horace grinned then, and whatever shadow had been there fled as quickly as it had come. "That's the spirit." He gestured toward the door, and the warehouse space beyond. "Same time tomorrow?"

"It'll be Raedrick's turn, but sure."

Horace chuckled, and Julian exited the office.

The chill of the open space struck him immediately, but he almost didn't notice it. He hurried across to the door to the street, not bothering to tuck his cloak about him.

He needed to see Jamie about that strongbox. Then he was going to see to figuring out what Hamel was up to.

14

TORGENS AND YARNEL

When Julian got back to the Constabulary, he found Raedrick there at his desk, frowning down at a stack of papers like they had just cursed his mother.

"That looks fun," Julian said, and pushed the door closed. He took a moment to doff his cloak and hang it on one of the hooks by the door, then clomped over to his desk. The warmth radiating from the wood stove in the corner behind his desk grew with each step, and by the time he settled himself down into his chair, he could barely remember the bone chill of the day outside.

Barely.

"What is that?" he said, gesturing at the pages that had Raedrick so thoroughly entertained.

Raedrick grunted and leaned back in his chair. "Inventory reports from the grocers association."

Julian raised an eyebrow at that. "Didn't we settle all that yesterday?"

"Well, they wanted to make double sure we had all the information we needed, I guess." Raedrick rolled his eyes to the ceiling, then focused in on Julian. "Where have you been this morning?"

"Made the rounds through the winter stores. No thieving in

the last day, you'll be happy to know." He put an extra bit of light-hearted inflection into it, but Raedrick didn't take the bait, he just grunted and nodded. "Then I figured I'd see what our friendly neighborhood bard was up to."

Raedrick's mouth tightened. "I was afraid of that. I heard about last night, you know."

Julian nodded. How to explain? He decided just to lay it all out, what he had experienced during Hamel's song. By the time he finished, Raedrick's expression had softened. A bit. If anything, he was looking at Julian with an expression of concern more than anything else.

"So that's it. I know you think I'm nuts, but there is something going on with that guy, something weird."

Raedrick sighed and looked away from him, toward the cell block door. "Melanie is starting to think the same way."

"Oh?"

Raedrick nodded, and his lips turned down again. "But I'm telling you, I don't like it. Hamel's been nothing but neighborly since he got here. Everyone likes him, and he's been good for business. If you two start causing trouble for him—"

"You know, Horace said about the same thing to me a couple hours ago."

"Did he. Well, he's always had good sense."

Julian leaned forward in his chair, fixing Raedrick with a direct stare. "You don't think it's odd that both you and he feel so protective of a person who's only been in town for two weeks?"

Raedrick opened his mouth to reply. Then he paused, and Julian could see his wheels turning for a moment. His frown deepened. "I'm not—"

The door opened and a blast of cold swept the stove's heat away for a second before their visitor closed it.

He was a young man, darker of skin than the majority of Lydelton's inhabitants, with black hair that flowed to his shoulders and yellow-brown eyes. He wore the white and yellow of the Healers Circle beneath a thick grey woolen cloak. Julian recognized him immediately: Willam, assistant to Ravi Sebastini, the head of the Healers Circle here in Lydelton.

"Ah good, you're both here," Willam said without preamble. "Master Sebastini requests that you come to the Circle at once."

"What has happened?" Raedrick said, practically springing from his chair.

"A group of men was found down near the Eastflow. Master Sebastini has been treating them for exposure and thought you would want to hear their story."

Julian rose as well, and retrieved his cloak.

The Healers Circle lay two blocks west of the Constabulary. On a warm summer day, the walk there would be leisurely, taking several minutes.

Today, Julian practically ran.

In a few more weeks, the accumulating snow and freezing temperatures would make such a feat impossible, even with crampons strapped to the bottom of his boots. But winter still was stretching its limbs before fully embracing Glimmer Vale in its grasp, so despite the recent snowfall the streets were relatively clear.

And in fact, the footing was improved, because the dirt that made up all the streets except for Lydelton's main street were solidified, frozen into a firm surface by the steadily decreasing temperature, so that not even a hint of mud or anything but sure footing remained beneath a man's boots.

He almost felt bad, out-pacing Raedrick and Willam to the Circle, except that he had only just started to warm up again and the icy fangs of the day's growing chill—strange since noon had only just passed—were nipping at him like a rabid dog from the moment he left the refuge of his office.

Still, as he drew to a halt in front of the Circle's front door and looked back at the other two, they weren't as far behind him as he might have thought; only a few paces. So maybe he hadn't quite run, though he felt like he had.

Raedrick had a look of amusement on his face, and arched an eyebrow at him as he came to a halt to Julian's left, and Julian returned it with a grin and a shrug of his shoulders.

Willam just pulled the door open without comment, and they stepped inside.

They found Master Sebastini in the guild house's largest treatment room, to the rear of their building. That room had a quartet of narrow beds spaced out on either side and a fireplace along the rear wall.

Two men were seated in chairs in front of the fireplace, which was roaring with a freshly-stoked fire fed by thickly-cut logs, sending waves of warmth radiating throughout the entire room. Despite that, the men were bundled in thick white and yellow blankets that were emblazoned with the Healers Circle's emblem, and both clutched steaming mugs in their hands as they stared into the fireplace's flames.

Another man was bundled up on the first bed to Julian's right. He, too, was wrapped in a blanket, but he was curled up almost into a ball, arms wrapped around himself and the blanket pulled tight so only his eyes shown forth from within.

The last patient also sat in a chair, but he was farther back from the fireplace, across from the bedridden man. He had a blanket more loosely wound around his body, but he had his left foot submerged in a bucket of water.

Ravi Sebastini was crouched down next to that man when Julian and Raedrick entered. He was elderly, thin and wrinkled, and stooped from what once would have been an impressive standing height. But Julian had never dared to think him frail, even before the incident that had seen him accompany himself and Raedrick up the tallest mountain in the Saddleback range to rescue a trapped traveler, almost a year ago.

When they entered, Sebastini looked up and stood, straightening his robes, again in the white and yellow of his guild. He nodded greeting quickly.

"Thank you for coming, Constables," Sebastini said. He gestured to the man next to him, then to the other three. "I thought you might want to talk with these gentlemen."

Raedrick stepped forward, focused on the man sitting next to Sebastini. "I remember you," he said. "You were with the last caravan that came through."

The man in the chair looked up, meeting Raedrick's gaze, and nodded.

He was maybe five years Raedrick's senior, with a thick brown beard that was beginning to go grey in streaks, and matching hair that was cut to just below his ears. Beneath the Healers Circle blanket, he had on a leather breastplate, stained black, and had on brown leggings and an off-white tunic beneath his armor. He looked to be well-muscled, and he had a scar on his right cheek; a security guard for the caravan, unless Julian missed his guess.

"Aye," the man said. "Jorus Hasburg. We met when Master Torgens checked in with you after we got situated."

Raedrick nodded. "You were the head of security." He looked from the man to Sebastini, then over at the other three for a moment. He raised his eyebrow at the guild master.

Sebastini said, "He's got a frostbit foot."

"May or may not end up keeping it," Jorus said, cackling out a bitter laugh at the end, and Sebastini nodded.

"I am optimistic, though." The old healer gestured toward the two by the fireplace. "They will be fine in a couple hours, once their bones are heated up. But him…" His gesture turned toward the man curled up in the bed. "Physically, he's sound, aside from chill and minor frostbite on his nose and two fingers."

Julian looked over at the man in the bed again. He saw that the man also had a steaming mug, like his two comrades by the fireplace, clutched between hands that seemed to be trying to crush it. He was shaking, but not like a man chilled, more like one who was convulsing, almost.

"So what's wrong with him?" Julian said, and Jorus snorted out another laugh, this one even more bitter-sounding.

"That's why I called you," Sebastini said.

Julian looked back at Jorus. "Hamel told us you ran into weather below Silver Falls."

Jorus perked up visibly upon hearing Hamel's name. "The bard? He made it back here then."

Raedrick nodded, and Jorus shook his head.

"He's smarter than the lot of us. When he turned back, a bunch of the boys thought he had the right of it, but Master Torgens wouldn't hear of it. The storm passed in a day, and he insisted we push on. Folks grumbled, but we did it."

He paused to taken a drink from his mug, then swallowed with a loud "Pah" of exhalation as the warmth of the fluid—Julian presumed it was tea—hit his throat.

After a moment, Jorus continued, "It was hard pushing through the snowfall that first morning, but by evening we'd descended a bit and the way became easier, and I thought maybe Master Torgens had the right of it, after all. Even the loudest complainers seemed cheerful around the campfire that night."

"So what went wrong?" Raedrick asked.

"Just before noon the next day, we were rounding a curve on the path. There must have been a frozen patch, or maybe the driver was just not paying attention. But all of a sudden I heard the pack horses on our supply wagon scream. I looked back, and the wagon was half off the trail, and it was dragging the horses off with it. The driver managed to jump off, but the wagon and the horses went over the side and down into the river at the bottom of the ravine."

Julian's mouth dropped open, and he cringed inwardly at the notion. He and Raedrick had traveled up Garret's Gorge on their journey to Lydelton, and he recalled a number of tight turns on the path, and how precipitous the drop-off was. In early Spring, when they'd come up, it wasn't all that bad, but even then there was still ice on the rocks and the path, especially as they got closer to Silver Falls.

At this time of the year, especially after a snowfall…treacherous would probably be the easiest way to describe it. Even still, the idea that a wagon and team could slide off like Jorus described… He shuddered to think of it.

"That wagon had all our food and sundries. Not the trade goods, much to Master Torgens's relief. But there were over a dozen of us, and only what food we had in our own saddlebags all the way to Calas."

Readrick whistled. "It took the two of us," he gestured from himself to Julian, "a bit more than two weeks to reach Silver Falls from Calas. But that was without wagons, and in the spring."

Jorus nodded. "Aye. We were looking at a good month, what with the wagons and the snow on the ground, and more probably coming." He drank again. "Well, all the lads who wanted to turn around when the bard left were up in arms now, and I couldn't blame them. Better to wait out the winter here than starve or freeze to death on the road. But Master Torgens wouldn't hear of it. I guess he'd had rough times lately, and had everything riding on this run. He refused to even think about turning around. Insisted that once we got below the tree line on west side of the pass we'd be fine. There would be small farmsteads we could buy supplies from to tide us over til Calas, and that was only a few days away."

He lowered his eyes, starting at his soaking foot for a moment. "He ordered me to string up anyone who talked about coming back."

"Did you?" Raedrick asked.

Jorus nodded slowly, not looking up. "Only took one. Busted his lip good, hogtied him, and threw him in the back of one of the wagons, and everyone else fell in line." He inhaled, and let out a little chuckle. "And you know what? For the next day or so it looked like Master Torgens was right."

"But then…" Julian said, letting the word trail off into a not-question.

"But then we woke up to snow up to mid-calf with more falling. And I mean falling. Flakes as big as a thumbnail, and blown on the wind so that we could barely see from one end of our camp to the other. Couldn't even begin to budge the wagons from where they were stuck, because as soon as we dug one wheel out, the others were snowed back in again. Even Master Torgens agreed there was nothing for it but to wait it out, and hope we could undig when the storm passed."

Jorus drew a long breath and shuddered. "Except it didn't. Three days it kept up, until the wagons were almost totally buried. And we could barely move from one tent to another."

Julian traded looks with Raedrick. "Thought you said the first snows had only just started coming in when I got back to town?"

Raedrick nodded. "Here, yes. But that side of the mountain range…" He shrugged. "Things can be different." He looked back at Jorus. "And obviously they were. So you decided to turn back after that. Where are the others?"

Jorus shook his head "Not so simple as that. Master Torgens still wanted to continue, or at least stay. He wouldn't hear of leaving his wagons to be picked over by passers-by." The look he gave Raedrick was grim. "He really must have sunk everything into this trip. Only way I can figure it. Anyway, them as wanted to leave were done listening, and frankly I was as well."

"You?" Julian said.

Jorus shrugged. "It's one thing to keep up order when there's a chance for a payoff. But at that point," he shook his head, "he'd lost it, completely. You should have seen his eyes when he realized we were going to leave. Wild, red-shot." He looked over at the man lying, quivering, on the bed. "Yarnel never saw it coming."

"That's Yarnel?" Raedrick looked over at the stricken man, then back at Jorus with a raised, questioning eyebrow.

Jorus shook his head again. "No, that's Hab. Yarnel's his

brother. Or was. First time away from the farm for both of 'em. Took jobs driving wagons, and off to see the world. I guess Master Torgens thought if he started to slitting throats, it wouldn't take long for us to fall in line, just like after I hogtied that fellow a couple days before. He grabbed Yarnel right in front of Hab, and…" Jorus shuddered. "When I finally pulled Hab off of Master Torgens, I couldn't tell if he had more of his brother's blood on him or Torgens's. Torgens wasn't quite dead, but there wasn't much we could do for him. And no one much wanted to."

"So you left him there." Raedrick said it flatly, and Jorus nodded.

"In a snowdrift pooling in his own blood." He looked back over at Hab. "When we reached the docks at the south end of the lake, most of the lads went down to that big ranch tucked away in the Hook. But I decided to bring Hab the rest of the way here." He shrugged again. "Thought you oughta know about what happened."

Julian looked back at Hab, still just lying and shaking on the bed. "So what happened to him?"

"Nothing. Just been staring into space, not saying nothing for the last week. One of the lads had to practically drag him up the trail."

"Gods be merciful," Julian said, and Jorus grunted.

15

INCARCERATION

aedrick and Julian exchanged looks, then Readrick gestured toward Master Sebastini, and then the door. The old healer, understanding, nodded and moved away.

"Thank you, Jorus," Raedrick said. "Do you need anything?"

Jorus shrugged, and made a wry grin. "Just an unfrozen foot, is all."

Julian and Raedrick met Sebastini in the hallway outside the treatment room. It was narrow, and dimly lit by a pair of oil lamps set in brass sconces at either end of the hall. The walls were bare wood that was darkly stained and made the passage seem almost oppressive.

"When will it be safe to move Hab from here?" Raedrick said, and Sebastini shrugged slightly.

"As I said, Constable, there is nothing wrong with him that I can see. Physically anyway."

Julian looked Raedrick askance. "You want to take him into custody?"

Raedrick nodded. "He killed a man in front of three witnesses."

"Right after that man killed his brother in front of all those witnesses. I'm not sure I can call that murder, Rae."

Raedrick pursed his lips, mulling it over for a moment. "I'm not sure I can either, but that's for the judge to determine."

Which was fair enough, Julian supposed. And probably correct, by the letter of the law. He sighed. "We just got Trevir out of the cell block, and now we're replacing him."

"And just in time for Amos's audit, also," Raedrick added.

Julian sighed again. "Well, let's get to it."

It took almost half an hour to get Hab moved over from the Healers Circle and situated. Mostly because he didn't cooperate at all. He didn't resist, he just…didn't move. Sat there like a lump, so in the end they had to enlist Willam's assistance in carrying him to the Constabulary.

A bit of huffing and puffing later, and Hab was lying on a cot in the center cell on the right hand side of the cell block, still shaking like he had been. It was almost like he hadn't even noticed the entire trip over, except that his face was reddened from the chill of the outside air.

"Well," Julian said as he closed and locked the cell. "Guess I'll get that stove lit." He nodded at the wood stove on the rear wall of the cell block, the sole source of heat for the lengthy room. Raedrick had doused it after releasing Trevir earlier in the day, and the space had already become quite chilled.

It only took a few moments to re-light the flame; many of the coals within the stove were still warm, and the stack of tinder and fuel logs adjacent to the stove were well seasoned. Soon enough there was a merry blaze within the cast iron of the stove, and he closed the fuel door and went back to the office.

Amos was at his desk, speaking with Raedrick, who had taken his own seat, when Julian emerged and paused to close and lock the cell block door.

"I've been thinking about that," Amos said. "There are a number of widows in town. Maybe we should hire them."

Julian hung the cell block door's key on the wrought iron ring that was driven into the door frame to hold it, and turned to look at Amos. "Hire them for what?"

Raedrick said, "Amos has been continuing his work on the prisoner meals issue."

"Ah." Julian slid over to his desk, and took a moment to throw another piece of fuel into the office's stove. As he did, he ran Amos' words over in his mind.

"That's not a bad idea, Rae," he said as he settled down into his chair. "A woman in those straights could use every extra bit of coin she can get."

Raedrick nodded, looking thoughtful as he also considered the idea. "That's true." He winced slightly and turned to meet Julian's look. "I'm ashamed we never thought of it before."

"Well you two were new to town, and you already knew Molli, right?" Amos said.

Julian nodded, and so did Raedrick, and the young man shrugged before continuing, "It was the easiest way to solve the problem, and it worked. Don't fix what isn't broken?"

"Yes, except it was," Raedrick said. "We just didn't see it." He leaned forward, pressing his elbows onto the top of his desk as he gave Amos his full attention. "What do you have in mind?"

Amos had the accounts ledger open on his desk, and had been writing on another piece of parchment beside it. He gestured toward the ledger. "I'm still not done with my audit, but it looks like you're averaging two prisoners a month, for two weeks each. That varies, of course. But I was thinking we could set up a rotation. One household could take a week at a time."

Julian pursed his lips, pondering, then shook his head. "That's a lot of work, especially if the woman has children to look after still."

Raedrick nodded. "Agreed. I think let's assign a different

person to a specific day of the week, and rotate that way. Less of an imposition on anyone's routine."

"Yeah, and that would also spread the money around more evenly among the ladies," Julian added.

Amos chewed on his lip for a moment, then nodded. "It would give me a bit more to coordinate, but it shouldn't be too hard, doing it that way." He paused, then said, "I've been thinking it through some more, and I think we should keep paying them the same as we're paying The Oarlock now."

Raedrick blinked. "I thought your whole point was to save money?"

Amos shrugged. "Well, if the mayor doesn't have any issue with the budget you've been using, maybe it doesn't matter. And it might look bad if you started paying widows less than you had been paying one of the larger businesses in town."

"Good point," Raedrick said.

"I don't see how the mayor could object. Brimly might have, but Stepan?" Julian shook his head. "He's not one to put on airs."

Raedrick looked Julian askance. "Mayor Brimly wouldn't have objected either."

"But he would have wanted to."

A pause, then Raedrick snorted out a half-chuckle. "You may be right. Alright, Amos," he said, "start looking to see who is able and interested in taking on the job. Once you've got a line-up ready, I'll break the news to Molli."

Julian leaned back in his chair and chuckled. "She won't even notice the difference, what with all the extra business Hamel's been bringing in."

What amusement there had been on Raedrick's face fled as if it had never been there, and he turned a serious gaze Julian's way. "And what has your favorite fellow been up to today? You said you followed him around this morning." There was disapproval in his tone, but it was more muted than it had been during their earlier discussion.

Julian shrugged. "Didn't follow him per se. Just checked in on him a few times." Raedrick's eyebrows raised, and Julian continued before he could interject. "But he wasn't up to much. Breakfast in The Oarlock and then he went to call on Povol."

Raedrick blinked. "Povol?"

Julian nodded. "I mentioned dog sledding to him yesterday and he seemed interested, so I pointed him Povol's way."

"I heard Povol had been training up a new team this summer," Raedrick mused. "Are they ready to go yet?"

"Guess so, because they made arrangements to journey out into the Glamorwood day after tomorrow."

Raedrick's expression grew questioning.

"I went in and asked Povol about it after Hamel left."

There was a long moment of silence, then Raedrick blew out a breath that reeked of annoyance. "Do you intend to continue stalking the man's every move? Because I have to tell you—"

"I know, I know. Folks won't like it, and neither will you, because he's so popular all of a sudden."

Raedrick just looked at him, a scowl growing on his lips. Then he rolled his eyes and looked up at the ceiling, as though he could stare through it to the gods themselves, to ask their mercy. "Fine, whatever. If it makes you feel better, do as you will. Just don't make a scene out of it."

"Rae, you know me better than that."

He gave Julian a wry look in return, but the semi-scowl was gone, replaced by an expression of fond amusement.

Then Raedrick stood from his chair and straightened his coat. He took a moment to look around the office, then nodded to himself. "Time for my afternoon rounds, then I'm going to check in on Lani and Celia." He glanced Julian's way. "I'll let you take care of the report to the judge about our new guest." He jerked a thumb toward the cell block door.

Julian blinked, then groaned. That paperwork was always painful; it was one of the chief things he'd enjoyed not having to deal with while he, Jared, and Melanie had been away.

Raedrick saw the look on his face and grinned broadly. "Consider it a welcome home present." And was there a bit of friendly, but sadistic, joy in that grin?

He walked over to the door and took his cloak off its peg, then donned it. As he was clasping the neck closed, he looked back at Julian. "After that, why don't you grab Jared and Melanie and bring them by for dinner? Lani is working on a new recipe, and she wants to try it out a bit before they start using it in The Oarlock."

That took a bit of the sting out of the paperwork deal. Still…

"You're just trying to keep me away from Hamel, aren't you?"

Raedrick's grin slipped slightly, and he shrugged. "Two birds with one stone."

Julian rolled his eyes, but nodded. "Have it your way. For tonight, anyway."

The grin re-expanded. "I thought you'd say that. See you at sundown." Then Raedrick stepped out into the chill of the afternoon. Before the door shut behind him, his cloak flashed red; he had activated the enchantment Melanie had placed into the cloak, to ward against the cold.

Julian considered that he ought to ask Melanie to make him one of those. It sure would make doing his rounds easier; almost pleasant. And that would be good for the town. Given that, maybe he could get the mayor to agree to pay for it? That way…

He realized he was just delaying the paperwork drudgery, and he pulled his thoughts back together, hard.

Then, with another sigh, he got to work.

16

SPICE ON THE TONGUE

Julian had to hand it to Lani; she was just as good a hand about the kitchen as her mother. Maybe better.

He had expected the new recipe to involve fish. Considering how much of the local economy was driven by the Covington Brothers, most meals in Lydelton had at least some amount of fish in them. But what he hadn't expected was a stew of fish chunks mixed with sliced sausages and a melody of vegetables in a creamy broth that teamed with spices that left his tongue sizzling as much from the cacophony of flavors as from heat.

Julian finished two full bowls and was mopping up the remains with a heel of bread in no time, to the amused look of Melanie, who was sitting across Raedrick and Lani's table from him, in a black dress with a deep red sash about her waist, that was snug at the bosom but loose in the sleeves.

"Are you going to come up for air any time soon?" she asked, an eyebrow arching meaningfully and a teasing lilt to her voice.

To his right, Jared chuckled, but Julian didn't bother responding. He bit into the bread and let the last of the stew's juices linger on his tongue for a moment before chewing—slowly—and swallowing.

He looked Melanie in the eye they whole time, grinning through his chewing, and after a moment, she looked up toward the ceiling and let out a sigh that sounded like it wanted to be a laugh, but refused to on general principle.

Raedrick was sitting to Julian's left. He had doffed his coat and was in his shirtsleeves, the laces at his neck loosened in the warmth thrown off by the stove that dominated the kitchen and eating chamber where they all sat. He laughed for real in response to Melanie's faux exasperation.

"Julian always gave the cooks fits when we were out on patrol," Raedrick said. "They never could manage to figure the right amount of supplies to bring, mostly on account of him."

Julian shrugged and stuffed the last of the bread into his mouth. "Gotta give that lot something to do."

Lani was seated to Melanie's right, across from Raedrick. She had on a light blue dress that was laced with grey thread. Celia was in her basket at the head of the table where either Lani or Raedrick could reach her easily. She looked at Julian appraisingly. "I suppose I don't have to ask whether you approve of the recipe or not."

He shrugged again. "Could use a little more salt."

She just looked at him for a long moment, then she, too, rolled her eyes to the ceiling. Then she looked back down at Jared. "What do you think?"

Jared had kept his coat on, like Julian. And he had dribbled a bit of the stew earlier, leaving a little stain on the right side of his chest. The grey-white broth stood out nicely against the bright red fabric.

"I think it's great," Jared said.

"You have truly outdone yourself, Lani," Melanie said, seriously.

Lani inclined her head in response, and Julian had the impression she was trying to put on a professional air. Problem was her beaming smile gave that all away. Had she truly been uncertain how they would take it?

"Yeah," he said. "I think you've got a hit on your hands. Only question is," he reached for the goblet in front of his plate. It was halfway filled with burgundy-colored fluid from the wine bottle Raedrick had opened when they sat down together. "Whether you'll be able to make enough to keep up with demand."

"Have you seen the size of their kettles?" Jared said. "I think they'll be fine."

Julian sipped at his wine, and let the fruity flavor, touched with a bit of acid, swish around in his mouth for a moment. Then, swallowing, he shrugged. "Hope so." He grinned Lani's way. "What are you calling it?"

"Farzal's Folly."

Julian blinked. "You're naming it after...*him*??"

Farzal was the leader of the brigand band that had been harassing Lydelton when Raedrick and Julian first arrived in Glimmer Vale, and he was the reason they were now constables of the town. He caused a lot of damage, and it took the town a long time to recover from his campaign of terror.

It helped everyone to know that he and Raedrick had sent Farzal to the gallows down in Mangin City. Except...he never made it there. He had somehow escaped while on his way to the Capital to make an appeal to the crown. After learning of his escape, Raedrick and Julian had decided not to spread the word; they only told the Mayor, and he'd agreed it would serve no purpose to alarm the people of Lydelton.

So hearing that Lani intended to name this bit of magic after him... Julian wasn't sure what to think about it.

"It's been almost two years," Lani said, "and I think it's time we acknowledge what happened," she stretched her hand across the table, and Raedrick squeezed it, "and what you two did for us." She inhaled quickly. "The spice reminds of the trouble that he brought, his hubris, and the losses we took. While the zest and the after-flavor calls to mind our victory, and the good times that followed."

"I...see." Julian looked from her toward Melanie. She had

fought by his and Raedrick's side, with her magics. As had a number of the fishing men and a few others in the town.

She had her lips pursed, as she mulled over Lani's words. Then she nodded, briskly. "A good name. The alliteration makes it flow easily on the tongue."

Everyone just looked at her, and Julian wondered if they were thinking the same thing he was: what was alliteration?

Finally, Raedrick said, "I also think the name is good."

"Big surprise," Julian said, and gave his old friend a wink. "Well," he looked back at Lani, "I guess you'll have a hit on your hands in more ways than one."

Nods all around, and they all drank from their goblets.

Silence lingered for a time, then Melanie cleared her throat. "Since it looks like we're done eating, I have something I need to discuss." She looked from Raedrick to Julian and back again, and her face grew businesslike, serious.

"Alright," Julian said, putting the question into the end of the word.

Instead of responding, Melanie pushed her chair back and stood. She took a breath to smooth the skirts of her dress, then went over to the front door of Raedrick and Lani's flat, to where she had hung her cloak and left a bulging leather satchel. Hefting the satchel, she returned to the table and set it down next to her— not quite completely empty—bowl.

Melanie undid the ties on her satchel and flipped the top open, revealing the spines of two thick, leather-bound books. She gave Raedrick a meaningful look. "I found what I was looking for earlier."

Raedrick's eyebrows rose. "Oh?"

She nodded, her eyes flicking toward Julian again for a second. "And I think Julian is right."

Raedrick frowned, but it was more thoughtful than anything else. "Show me."

Lani looked at the satchel and its two large tomes on the

already-cluttered table, and shook her head. "Let's get these dishes cleared away first."

17

LIGHT READING

It didn't take long to clear the table, with all of them helping, and then Lani pulled out a rag and shooed Julian and Raedrick away from the kitchen area, and back to Melanie. But when Jared moved to join them, he found himself hauled back to her side.

As Julian settled himself back down in his chair across from Melanie, he couldn't help but chuckle at Jared's protests as he found himself elbows-deep in dirty dishes.

Melanie wasted no time, but pulled the two books out. The first, the thicker and obviously older of the two, she set down on the middled of the table, then she cracked it open and spun it around so the text was facing Raedrick and Julian.

"Do you remember this?" she asked.

Raedrick nodded. "That's the history that told you about Kalem and the Falconer's Stairs."

Melanie nodded. "Written by one of Botreaus Hevergod's warlord rivals. You will recall it mentioned Hevergod's power in matters magical, and that of the sorcerers who followed him. Well, it also mentions something else. I didn't think much of it at the time when I first read it; I was more concerned with learning about who Kalem was. But what you said," she raised an eyebrow at Julian, "the other night, and what we both experienced last night—"

"What do you mean, what *we* experienced?"

She told him quickly, and he felt his eyebrows raising high onto his forehead.

Melanie continued before he could say anything. "As I was thinking about it last night, and again this morning, it sparked a memory. In here."

She tapped a paragraph on the left hand page. Julian leaned forward to see it more closely. He had to squint a bit in the relatively dim light of Raedrick's oil lamps; the script was small and tightly-written. But after a minute, he was able to make it out.

After the first day of battle, we felt certain of defeat. The Butcher and his sorcerers harried our troops all day, and we took many losses. Even after both armies withdrew for the night, they continued their harassment. Ghostly lights moving in the shadows around the camp, accompanied by frightful noises, greeted our sentries, and prevented most of the remainder from getting anything but a fitful, distressing sleep.

Julian stopped his reading and looked up at Melanie. "That sounds familiar," he said. It was very familiar; they and Jared had experienced something almost identical in their first night below the Falconer's Stairs.

Melanie nodded. "I thought it would. Read on."

We were in no condition for battle the next day, and the Butcher knew it. His army advanced, and we were forced to flee. All day, his sorcerers harassed our march, until by evening we had lost a tenth of our remaining men, left behind with wounds too grievous to treat without impeding our flight. The remainder of our men were dropping with exhaustion, and there was rumbling in the ranks. I felt certain the men would mutiny, or just flee in the darkness.

Throughout the campaign, I had made it a practice to detain any passers-by who might inform the Butcher of our movements until after we had passed well clear, and shortly before we finished making camp, our forward scouts escorted in a traveling band of performers that they had intercepted earlier in the afternoon. In an effort to stave off the cata-

strophe of morale that I saw building up, I ordered them dispersed throughout the camp to perform as best they could.

The difference between that night and the previous was dramatic. Spirits buoyed immensely, far beyond my wildest hopes. And though the lights and the noises returned, they were muted, easily ignored until, shortly before midnight, they ceased completely, and the men were able to rest.

Julian whistled slowly, and looked up at Raedrick.

He didn't seem very impressed as he raised his own eyes from the page. "A little morale boost can go a long way, more than you would imagine," he said. "In those kinds of situations, it can feel like a floating log to a drowning man."

Melanie nodded. "I have no doubt. But it reads like more than a morale boost. The magical attacks from the previous night were thwarted."

Raedrick shook his head. "By minstrels? I highly doubt that. Hevergod's troops would have been tired also, especially his sorcerers. They probably detached fewer of them on the harassing detail the second night, and when they saw their efforts weren't being as effective they decided to abort and conserve their strength."

A little shrug and a half-nod, and Melanie closed the book and pulled it back to herself. "That could be the case. But it's not all I found." She opened the second book and flipped to a page two-thirds of the way to its end.

"This," she said, "is part of the memoir of a scholar named Rezany. He lived around the turn of this century, and traveled extensively for his research. Here," she spun the book to face them, "he writes of his time in the Hermelite Empire."

That name sent a little shiver down Julian's spine. He and Raedrick spent many weeks on the front lines of the Kingdom's war against that same Empire, and they were not fond memories.

"What sort of research?" Raedrick asked.

"He was an historian. He spent decades ferreting out fact from folklore and legend, so as to complete a definitive work on the history of the continent for the Royal Museum."

"Did he succeed?" Julian asked.

Melanie shook her head. "Alas, no. He died before finishing his work. He left copious notes, but changes in policy and funding priorities meant that after he was gone, with no one to fight for it, the project went fallow. No one picked up where he left off." She frowned as she looked down at the book. "It's a shame. I managed to read one of his completed volumes in the museum when I was in the Capital, and it was excellent. So much that when I came across this, I could not resist snatching it up."

She pointed down at the top paragraph on the right-hand page. "Start here."

Julian leaned in.

Hermelite ascetics have a centuries-old musical tradition, combining throat-singing chants with a sort of bowed multi-string organ. Several dozen strings are suspended in a device that runs the length of the meditation chamber. Half a dozen men use horsehair bows, under the coordination of an organ conductor, to play intricate harmonies that match and augment the vocal chanting. The overall effect is magnificent; I have never heard its like.

It is also said to be healing. Pilgrims have been known to travel hundreds of miles just to sit in the meditation chamber for a few hours, and it is said that many have maladies cured that had been plaguing them for years.

Surely this must be just folklore and rumor. That was my assumption.

But I myself witnessed a man hobbling into the chamber on a crutch. The monks who escorted him told me his knee had been ruined in a rock slide when he was ten years old. I swear by all the gods, after sitting there for most of the day, I saw him walk out without any need of the crutch at all.

It was like a sort of magic.

Melanie's eyes burrowed into Julian's. "Like a sort of magic."

Julian nodded eagerly, his spirits buoying. "Yeah, that's what it was. Something in the notes or the way he played…" He turned to Raedrick and pointed an index finger at him. "I told you he was up to something."

Raedrick raised his hands, palms out, and shook his head. "Hold on now. This is talking about a room-sized thing played by how many people? And Hamel is one man with a harp. And besides, maybe that fellow wasn't really healed, he just thought he was for a while. Or this Rezany made it up."

Melanie snorted softly. "He was a very well-respected scholar, Raedrick. Such men do not fabricate facts." Raedrick opened his mouth to retort but Melanie held up a hand to forestall him. "But I'll grant the situation here is much different than what he describes. Still, given what's been happening… I don't think we can rule it out."

"Nothing's been happening, except to you two," Raedrick replied, a bit of heat in his words. "No one else had any problem the entire time Hamel's been here."

Melanie nodded, conceding the point. "It may be that he's been doing it ever since he arrived, and over the weeks the rest of you have become accustomed to it, so you don't even notice the effects. Or if you do, it just seems normal, not worth noting."

Raedrick frowned, pondering, then he shook his head. "Then Jared would have noticed something, but he hasn't." He looked over to the kitchen area, where Jared and Lani were finishing up. Jared was wiping his hands, wet from the cleanup, on his leggings. "Have you, Jared?"

"Have I what?" Jared said, stepping back to the table.

"Have you noticed anything odd around our new friend Hamel?"

Jared shrugged and took his seat again. He grinned good-humoredly at Julian and cuffed him on the shoulder lightly. "You mean like mister dreamy here?" He shook his head. "No, like I said the other day, it just seemed like good music to dance to, to me." His grin grew more broad, lusty. "Really got the blood pumping, you know? Why, you remember Gertrude, the seamstress, who I thought might be sweet on me, back before we left?"

Raedrick nodded, raising a questioning eyebrow.

"Well after that first dance, I decided what was I waiting for, an invitation, so I asked her for a turn." He waggled his eyebrows. "Turns out she's really, really sweet on me. It was a good night, and we're seeing each other again tomorrow."

Melanie gave him a level look. "I don't think we really need the details, Jared," she said. "But," she narrowed her eyes slightly, "you never considered asking her before?"

Jared shrugged. "Considered? Yeah. But I wasn't really sure if I was imagining things, so…" He spread his hands.

"So what made you decide to take the risk the other night?"

He shrugged again. "I dunno. Like I said, my blood was pumping, and it seemed like I was being a fool to worry over it. And anyway, she looked at me as I went past her table, and…well, it was obvious she wanted to have a turn, you know?"

"Hmm." Melanie pondered for a moment, then turned back to Raedrick. "I think Jared *was* affected. Just not as…profoundly…as Julian and I were."

Raedrick looked doubtful. Very doubtful.

"Well," Melanie said, "there is a way to know for sure."

"Oh?" Julian said. "How?"

"All magic is a transfer of energy. For the magic practiced in the Magestirium, the energy from the destruction of the components fuels the magical effects. It may be that Hamel's magic," Raedrick opened his mouth to speak, but she went on quickly, "if indeed it is magic at all and not our imagination, draws its energy straight from him. Or rather, from the energy of the music he plays. I know of a spell that makes magical energy and effects visible, to the practitioner who casts it, for a short time."

Julian blinked, surprised. "That's a thing?"

Melanie nodded. "It is not used often, usually only to confirm enchantments on magical items and the like. But if Hamel's music is somehow creating a magical effect, that spell should reveal it."

She looked at Raedrick and raised an eyebrow. "However, it's not easy to cast, and the components required are quite expensive. I only have enough for one casting, maybe two."

"Are you asking me to reimburse you?"

"Why Raedrick, whatever do you think of me? I'm not asking *you* for anything. The office of the Constable, however..." She put on a sly smile. "Surely this is a public service, after all."

He snorted out a laugh, but nodded. "If it turns out that he has been putting a spell on all of us, I guess it is." What humor was carried in that laugh faded quickly as the import of his words landed, and he frowned.

Julian did as well. "I almost hope not, and that I'm just going crazy."

Raedrick looked sidelong at him. "I'm afraid that ship sailed a long time ago, my friend."

It was meant to be funny, Julian knew. But right then, it didn't land. He just nodded.

"Well," Melanie said, closing the book. "Tomorrow night, when he plays in The Oarlock again, we'll find out."

18

A NOTE OF MAGIC

Melanie didn't feel any different. She wasn't sure if she really expected to, but when she completed the detection spell, it seemed as though something should have changed. Something at all.

But no, it was as though the spell did nothing, and she had just wasted the time chanting out a not-exactly-melodious incantation to no effect. Except the components had been exhausted, crumbling to dust in a little puff of smoke, like always.

So she gathered her wits and her cloak and hurried over to The Oarlock.

It was past sunset, and the stars stood out like tiny, twinkling beacons in the black of a near-cloudless night. The cold bit into her as she hurried the blocks from her home to the inn, a breeze from the north adding an extra bit of sharpness to its cut, and she pulled her cloak tight against it.

She should have made more than one of those brooches she gave Raedrick, she thought, and not for the first time.

But her strongbox was still stretched from the expense of that present, half a year or more from his and Lani's wedding. Or it had been, until Feirhard's gift. And she lacked some of the necessary components, so she couldn't have made another of them if she wanted to. And right that moment, she really wanted to.

And not just because having it would have immediately given assurance that the spell actually worked.

Well, soon enough.

The Oarlock's stable yard was well-lit by lamps at the sides of its entrance, and from the glow of firelight emanating through the windows at the front of the building itself. Off to the left, two men, the stable hands she supposed, sat on short stools that were pulled up to a small metal firebox. They were chatting in voices that didn't carry to Melanie's ears, but from the rapid puffs of mist from each of them, the talk was heated. Or at least fast-paced.

She didn't envy them their jobs, not on this night.

Warmth washed over her as she stepped inside, and she took a moment just to bask in it; both fireplaces were lit, and it felt glorious for a moment. Then the rest of the scene within registered, and enjoyment faded beneath anticipation of the evening's experiment.

The room was nearly completely full. Melanie could see individual empty chairs and stools here and there, but they were few, eclipsed by the throng of townspeople who had come to hear Hamel play. The crowd was about half fishing men and their families, from the grey cloaks they wore, but the other half was a cross-section of every trade and station in life that Lydelton had to offer.

The Oarlock usually did good, steady business, but Melanie could not recall seeing the place so packed in the past. It spoke to the high level of Hamel's musical talent.

And maybe to more.

Part of Melanie agreed with Julian from earlier; hoped that her suspicion was wrong, and there really wasn't anything more to Hamel and his appeal than his skill. But the rest of her didn't think that would really end up being the case.

It took two sweeps across the room before she spotted Raedrick and Julian. They were seated in one of the booths against left-hand wall across from the bar. The men were sitting next to each other, facing the entrance and the performance stage, but Melanie could see the golden locks of the back of Lani's head across from Raedrick.

She moved quickly, threading her way between the various tables and their bantering inhabitants, and twice had to stop to avoid running into servings girls hurrying about their duties. But then she was clear of the last table and drew up next to their booth.

Raedrick had doffed his cloak; it was hanging from a hook driven into the end of the booth's seat. The cloth was doubled over itself though, so she couldn't see the brooch.

"Hello, Melanie," Lani said, bobbing her head in greeting as the men stopped talking to each other and turned to face her.

"Good evening," Melanie said, and reached out to Raedrick's cloak. The folds parted easily beneath her fingers, and she felt a bit of tension for a moment.

She had never used this spell before, and didn't know what to—

Her breath caught in her throat as the brooch came into view. It looked completely normal, no change at all from the last time she'd seen it. But there was...something...else. An ephemeral shimmer, almost a glow, that seemed to surround it, like the glow was wafting out and then fading within less than a hand's width. It was slightly white of golden, and wispy, seeming to flow and pulse like a thing alive.

And Melanie supposed that in a way, it was. Magic was merely a changing of energy from one form—in her spells, the material of the components used—into something else that could be put to useful effect. For this brooch, she had imparted enough of that altered energy into it that it lingered, so Raedrick would be able to use its warming effects for probably several years.

She wasn't actually sure how long it would be until that energy ran out, but it would be at least that long.

All that flashed through her mind in a heartbeat, replaced by a mixture of relief and anticipation. Relief that the spell worked as advertised, and anticipation of finally putting the Hamel question to rest.

"You ok, Melanie?" Julian asked from his seat, against the wall, opposite Raedrick from her. "You look like something jumped up and bit you."

She blinked and looked back over at her friends, then nodded. "Yes, fine. Just…" She let go of the cloak's folds, letting it go back to hanging naturally. "I wasn't sure how the spell would work."

Raedrick cocked an eyebrow at her. "You cast it already?"

"It is not a simple incantation. I wouldn't have been able to perform it here." She saw another question forming on his lips. "But you needn't worry. Its effect should last an hour or so. Plenty of time."

Raedrick nodded and traded a glance with Lani, across from him. She had Celia, of course, but this evening the baby was swaddled in a sort of sash that Lani wore from left shoulder to right hip. It looked a comfy, convenient way to carry the child.

And probably easy for letting her eat.

Without Celia's usual basket, Lani had that side of the booth to herself, so Melanie moved to join her.

But Raedrick shook his head. "You'll need to see him, right?" He slid out of his spot and settled in next to Lani, who shifted over to give him more room. Then he grinned. "Besides, it's more comfortable here," he said, and he nudged Lani lightly and took her hand in his.

"Indeed," Melanie said as she sat in his former spot, not at all feeling a flash of envy for even that small show of intimacy. It had been a long time since Timon, after all.

But that wasn't her business tonight, was it?

As if on cue, she felt Julian's elbow, and he gestured toward the other side of the room. "There he is."

All eyes turned toward the rear end of the bar, where Hamel, dressed in his green coat again, was engaged in conversation with Molli. The greying innkeeper was beaming ear to ear, her head bobbing up and down in agreement with something Hamel said. Then the two parted ways as he hefted his harp case and made his way toward the performance stage.

The crowd noted his arrival in stages, a hush seeming to flow out from him through the gathered people as conversations stopped and all eyes turned to watch him. There was a feeling of expectation in the air, palpable so that Melanie could almost touch it, as Hamel reached the stage.

He was silent for a short while, un-casing his harp and getting situated on the stool that had been left for him. He plucked at the strings a few times, she assumed as a final test of the tuning, then he took a breath and looked out at the crowd, beaming a smile.

That smile flickered briefly as he stopped his gaze on a table a bit off to his right. It came back to full just as quickly as it faltered, though, so the hiccup was only barely noticeable.

"My friends," he said, loudly enough to carry easily to every ear, "we have new additions tonight. Older friends of mine," he gestured toward the table where his eyes had alighted, hand open and palm up as though presenting them to the crowd, though none of the people at the table were standing and Melanie couldn't make them out over the other people sitting between herself and them.

"These gentlemen were in the caravan I traveled with, and have just come through a harrowing experience," Hamel said, and a murmur spread through the crowd.

Word had circulated about the caravan's misfortune; Melanie had heard several people talking about it during the day. But clearly no one expected any of the harried men to be out from under the Healers Circle's care so soon.

"Since they'll be here all winter as well, I hope you'll welcome them as warmly as you have welcomed me." Hamel's eyes swept over the crowd again before coming back to rest on the table in question. "Gentlemen, your drinks are on me."

Someone at that table made a little whoop of appreciation, and Hamel grinned all the broader. "And this song is for you."

He began playing then, a jaunty and vigorous melody that took Melanie to a place of warmth and comfort, but more than that, of joyful play. Like one of the summertime festivals in the town where she'd grown up, when the people would string up lines between the buildings draped with colorful pennants, and the the entire populace would join for a feast followed by music, gaiety, and dancing the entire evening until well after sundown; almost to midnight.

Though she always felt constrained, shut-in, by the smallness of her ancestral home, Melanie had nonetheless loved those festivals. Being out in the warmth of the evening and feeling it drop to comfortable coolness even as the blood pumping in her veins from the exertion of the dance made her feel all the warmer. The rhythm of the music, the feel of companionship among her kin. The excitement of her first kiss, off in the shadows beneath the great oak that grew off to the side of the festival's staging.

The memories of those days flowed through her, bringing an inner warmth and a sense of happiness. But it was also tinged with a hint of regret; she hadn't realized how much she missed those festivals. Hadn't thought of them in years, actually.

Not since…

The crowd was clapping in rhythm with Hamel's playing, and with a start she realized he was also singing, a jolly verse that made laughter sweep through the room. Melanie found she wanted to laugh along with them.

But then she saw it.

It was subtle, easy to miss in the yellow-amber glow of the fireplaces and the softer glow of the oil lamps on the walls. And at first she thought it wasn't anything at all.

Then a particularly brisk arpeggio came, and it was plain to see, intensifying in time with the energy of the notes.

It was not like the glow surrounding Raedrick's brooch. It was more spread out, almost like a web of golden-white threads, carried on a wave. At each note Hamel plucked, each word he sang, the wave seemed to pulse, and the threads pressed outward, flowing over and around and through the crowded room, touching all.

Impacting all.

A chilly shiver went up her spine, counterpoint to the warm happiness that the music—that the magic—Hamel was weaving had evoked just a moment ago. And she swallowed against a suddenly dry mouth.

She looked across the table toward Raedrick and Lani.

They were still seated, but it seemed as if they were dancing in their seats, the way they swayed in time with the music.

Beside her, Julian was doing similarly, and tapping out the rhythm of the song with his palms on the tabletop in front of him.

Raedrick looked away from Lani toward her, smiling from the fun of it all, and stopped when he saw her. Her sudden realization must have shown on her face, because he raised a questioning eyebrow at her.

"Is he...?" he asked, clearly reluctant to voice the question out loud.

She nodded.

His smiled faded, his face hardening, and he turned in his seat to look Hamel's way.

Julian stopped tapping, his expression compressing into a look Melanie had come to recognize; it meant he was preparing himself for a fight soon to come.

"I knew it," he said. He looked at Raedrick, and the two men seemed to communicate without speaking.

After a few seconds, Raedrick said, "Too much ruckus if we do it tonight." He looked back at Hamel. "In the morning."

Julian nodded as well.

In the morning.

19

KNOWLEDGE AND CONSENT

Raedrick met Melanie and Julian in the common room of The Oarlock just after breakfast. He had donned his black coat and leggings, and his black boots, and had on a white ruffled shirt below the coat. Lani always said it was his most official, means business, look, and he tended to agree.

Julian was in green and grey, and had his new short sword on his hip instead of his longer blade. Melanie wore a bright blue dress with silver trim at the bodice and hems, and had her hair pulled back from her face with a silver band. She had her satchel containing the two tomes she had referenced the other night, and her usual knife balancing a pouch of her magical components on her belt, which was black with a silver clasp.

A very official-looking party, by design.

They gathered at the foot of the stairs for a moment, long enough to confirm with one of the serving girls that Hamel was still in his rooms, then the others followed him up.

He knocked quickly but firmly on the door, and had a flashback to the time almost two years ago when he and Julian had come to this very same door to enlist Melanie's aid against Farzal and his gang.

"Amazing the difference a couple years makes," he said to himself as he waited for Hamel to respond.

Melanie sniffed. "I was just thinking the same thing." She looked at the door with something akin to wistfulness for a moment. "I rather liked these rooms."

Raedrick chuckled softly at her echo of his own thought. But he quickly wiped that bit of humor from his expression when he heard the door's latch shift.

Hamel pulled the door open, and smiled a greeting when he saw them. "Constables. And Mistress Klemins! What can I do for you this morning?"

If he was troubled by their sudden appearance at his door, he didn't show it. If anything, he looked the epitome of poise, almost like he was ready to go up on the stage. He had on a bright blue tunic that puffed out a bit at the forearm and was unlaced at the collar, exposing the upper part of his chest muscles, and light brown leggings that were tucked into slightly darker calf-high, turned down boots. His hair was loose, spilling about his shoulders freely, but it looked as though it had been thoroughly combed. His eyes twinkled in the mixture of lamplight and early morning sun that shown in through the windows at the ends of the hallway and in the suite beyond.

"We'd like to talk to you, Hamel," Raedrick said, keeping his tone polite but businesslike.

The smile faded from the bard's face a bit, and his eyes danced between the three of them for a moment before settling fully on Raedrick.

"Is there a problem?"

"May we come in?"

Hamel shrugged and stepped back from the door, gesturing for them to enter.

Molli hadn't changed the furnishings in this room at all since the first time Raedrick had been in here. The suite had two chambers: the sitting room that they filed into and an adjoining bed chamber. The sitting room had a couch along the left-hand wall and two single chairs facing it across from a low, darkly-stained wooden table. A short bookshelf adorned one wall, and the other held a cabinet atop which was a decanter and a trio of clear glasses. An equal number of wine bottles, from the best vintage Molli carried, stood adjacent to the decanter. One of the bottles was half empty, its deep red contents filling the decanter a third of the way, so the wine could breathe.

Raedrick led the way to the couch and sat down, Julian beside him. Melanie took the chair closest the door. Hamel hesitated, then, shrugging again, settled down into the remaining one.

Then he leaned forward, resting his elbows on his knees, and raised an inquiring eyebrow at Raedrick.

"We know what you've been up to," Julian said.

Inwardly, Raedrick winced. He had planned to be more diplomatic about it, to lead up to the accusation.

But then he noticed Hamel's eyes widen ever so slightly, and he shoved that misgiving aside. Julian's direct approach had unsettled him, so maybe that was the right way after all.

"I beg your pardon?" the bard said.

"We've noticed the effect you've been having on the people of this town," Raedrick said, carefully not putting the accusation into his tone that Julian had. "I didn't think much of it at first. You're new, and stuck here for longer than you intended. So naturally you'd want to ingratiate yourself with us."

"Aye. I had planned to be in Calas by now, a cosmopolitan city. Not spending the winter in, no offense, a tiny village in the middle of nowhere. You have no idea how much coin I'm missing out on. And I know how things tend to work in small towns, when it comes to strangers. Can you blame me wanting to get on people's good side?"

Raedrick nodded slowly. "No, of course not. I would do the same in your shoes. It's," he leaned forward, narrowing his eyes at the bard, "the *way* you're going about it that concerns us."

Hamel's expression became guarded, like he wasn't certain what Raedrick was getting at, or dreaded it. Or both.

"I sing and play, and I socialize with the people."

"That's not all you do," Julian said.

"Are all graduates of the Morested Academy able to cast spells with their music, or is it just you?" Melanie interjected, and Hamel stopped moving. His eyes flickered between them, and Raedrick saw his lip tremble slightly for a moment.

The moment passed as quickly as it came, and Hamel laughed, sinking backward into the cushions of his chair in apparent amusement.

"I've heard my music called many things. Talented. Genius. Virtuoso. But never magical!" He waggled his eyebrows at Melanie. "I'll have to remember that, to seed into the crowd before I play my next venue. Alas, it's too late for this place. But the next will eat it up!"

Melanie's lips twitched upward slightly, in amusement Raedrick thought. But she didn't retort, she merely took the tomes from out of her satchel and placed them down on the table.

"These," she said, "point to the long-standing practice of, for lack of a better term, music magic, both here in the Kingdom and elsewhere."

"Fascinating," Hamel replied, but some of the amusement left his voice.

Melanie nodded. "It is. But it is not spoken of, at least not openly, even in the Magestirium."

"I imagine you would know more about that than I," the bard said, "given your history."

Melanie had opened her mouth to continue, but stopped at Hamel's words. Her brow furrowed, and Hamel shrugged.

"It's a small town, Mistress Klemins. People talk freely about the woman who openly flaunts the law of the King by dabbling in matters forbidden to all but the Magestirium." He looked away from her toward Julian, then Raedrick. "As they also tell of the men who deserted the army, yet somehow ended up as constables, despite being criminals themselves."

Julian shifted in his seat, and from the corner of his eye Raedrick could see a scowl beginning to form on his face. He could relate, but at the same time he had to admit it was a good play for Hamel to make.

I have my secrets, yes. But you have yours as well. Don't make an issue of mine and I won't make one of yours.

A nice play, if he would have tried to make it a year ago, before Melanie had made her arrangement with Vigilant Haversted and before he and Julian had come to an understanding with Marshal Leminster. Now, however…that implied threat rang hollow.

Very hollow.

"Nice try," Julian said.

Melanie's little smile returned, a tad larger than before. "You already know about me, so that will make this easier." She seemed to settle in her chair, like she was taking her ease while also presenting an aura of poised control. "You studied in the Capital. Surely you learned that those who practice the Magestirium's art are able to detect the presence of magics nearby." Her eyebrows rose. "The web you wove last night was…intriguing."

Hamel didn't reply, just looked at her. Raedrick could see the wheels turning behind the bard's eyes as he processed what she said.

"How does it work, precisely? Does the effect vary depending on the song: the melody and lyrics, the emotional content? Or can you evoke whatever effect you desire, regardless of what you are playing?"

"And what exactly are you trying to get us to do with it?" Julian added.

Hamel sniffed, and shook his head at Julian. "Not a thing, except to continue to welcome me here until the snows thaw at the end of winter."

"You expect us to believe that, after what you've been doing?"

Hamel rolled his eyes. "What exactly have I been doing? Making people's evenings more entertaining, spreading good cheer as the days grow shorter?" He snorted. "How sinister."

"It could be," Raedrick said.

Hamel shook his head. "Whatever it is you," he glanced at Melanie quickly, "*think* you know, I have committed no crime, caused no trouble for anyone since I've been here. So if you'll excuse me," he rose to his feet, "I have an appointment with Master Povol this morning." He flashed a grin Julian's way. "The dog sledding you mentioned the other day. It promises to be exhilarating, and I must finish getting ready."

The three of them traded looks. There was irritation on Julian's face, a mixture of amusement and something else that Raedrick couldn't quite place on Melanie's.

"Magicking people without their knowledge or consent isn't a crime?" Julian asked.

Hamel shrugged. "If you have *evidence* that will satisfy a judge," he extended his hands toward Julian, wrists together as though ready to receive shackles, "by all means take me in."

The challenge was there, plain as day, and Raedrick had to admit he could not answer it. All they really had was Melanie's word against Hamel's. That and Julian's description of his own experience. But nothing about what Julian felt could directly point at Hamel, and while Raedrick trusted Melanie implicitly, one word against another wasn't exactly rock solid.

Hamel was right; there was no way the judge would agree there was a case to proceed on, not the way things stood right then.

Raedrick rose to his feet and fixed Hamel with a serious look. "We will be keeping an eye on you, Hamel."

"I certainly hope so. I am, after all, now a resident of Lydelton." He chuckled. "At least until the snows thaw."

And therefore under your protection, Hamel didn't say. He didn't have to.

Raedrick nodded. "Enjoy your dog sledding."

Melanie and Julian had stood as well. They followed Raedrick back out into the hall, Melanie pausing only to pick her books back up.

As Hamel closed the door behind them, Julian sighed. "That could have gone...better."

❧ 20 ❧

TAKING STOCK

The walk back to the Constabulary was quiet. Julian and Melanie followed behind Raedrick, neither speaking as the trio made their way up to the paved Main Street and then a block further to the building that had been Raedrick's second home for so long.

He almost didn't notice the difference between the raw dirt of the side streets and Main Street's stonework; the ongoing chill in the air had solidified the dirt so that Raedrick was sure it would be extremely difficult to shovel through. And winter was only just beginning to set in. Soon the dirt would be hard as stone, of its own accord.

The leavings of the previous days' snowfall had mostly been pushed aside by the people's passage, aided by the toil of some of the men who worked in the mountains surrounding the vale, many of whom took up the job of clearing streets during the winter. So the going wasn't too difficult.

But soon that would change as well, requiring crampons strapped to the bottom of one's boots.

Not today, at least.

It was overcast, the light dim from the oppressive, low-hanging clouds overhead, and the breeze was fitful, out of the north. It carried the scent of woodsmoke from the various chimneys in town, but Raedrick detected something else beneath that.

"Snow's coming again," Julian said as they stepped off of Main Street and approached their building, and Raedrick grunted agreement.

There was a group of men standing on the Constabulary's porch as Raedrick, Julian, and Melanie arrived. They were bundled up in furs from head to toe, but Raedrick recognized them immediately: Jorus, and the other two caravan men who had been in the care of the Healers Circle.

They turned as Raedrick's group approached, and Jorus stepped forward to meet them.

"I'm surprised to see you up and about," Raedrick said after clasping hands with him. "How's the foot?"

Jorus shrugged. "Just about good as new." He grinned. "That Master Sebastini is a wonder, Constable. I wouldn'ta thought I'd ever walk on it again, but..." He raised the previously-stricken foot and made a little circle in the air with his boot, from the ankle.

Raedrick nodded. "Glad to see it." He looked from Jorus to his fellows. "What can we do for you?"

"We wanted to check in on Hab, if that's alright with you, Constable," one of the other men said. "Is he any better?"

"No change that I've seen yet." He frowned slightly. "Why didn't you just go in? You don't need to re-catch chill."

Jorus gestured toward the front door. "Door's locked."

"What?" Julian said. He stepped up to Raedrick's side, looking confused. And concerned.

Raedrick shared the sentiment. They hadn't come here yet this morning, instead meeting directly at The Oarlock. But Amos should have opened up for the day by now, and seen to Hab's breakfast at least.

Julian fished in his coat pocket for the key, and a moment later he had the door open, and Raedrick led the way inside.

It was dim, and chilly. The oil lamps were not lit, and the front office's stove had all but burned out. Only a faint orange glow from residual embers could be see through the little grates in the top of its face.

The cell block door was closed, and locked as well, and past it the cell block was even dimmer than the office so that he could barely make out any details within.

"Where is Amos?" Julian said as he bent over the stove and opened its fuel door. He took a poker that was leaning up against the stove's side and stirred up the embers, sending a few meager sparks flying, then added a few of the smaller pieces of fuel from the stack that was laid out beside the stove.

Raedrick didn't reply, instead he grabbed the cell block key from its hook and opened it, then stepped within.

It was less well lit than the office, but was actually more warm. Through the grates in the stove at the rear of the block, a brighter glow shown. But still the fire had dwindled down to nearly nothing, and he took a moment to stir it and add more fuel before he looked in on Hab.

The prisoner was laid out on his cot just about the same as he had been last night, when Raedrick checked on him before going home for the night after Hamel's performance. Except he was on his left side now, not his right.

And there was an odor emanating from the cell's bucket that said Hab had used it at some point. So he was not completely gone in the head; there was that proof, at least.

He re-lit the oil lamps, then looked forward toward the office, where the guardsmen waited, watching just past the barred entryway to the cell block.

Raedrick gestured for them to enter, and they filed in, meeting him before the bars of Hab's cell. They looked at him, frowning, and Raedrick said, "As you can see, not much change."

Jorus nodded slowly. "He said anything?"

Raedrick shook his head. "Just a word or two here and there, nothing that adds up." He stepped away from the cell. "Maybe he'll say something to you fellows. You know him better. Take as much time as you need."

When he came back into the office, he found Julian seated behind his desk. Melanie had scooted one of the guest chairs from the wall near the front door and was seated across Julian's desk from him.

"—won't be able to do that," she was saying.

"Do what?" Raedrick asked, and she looked his way.

"I won't be able to use the detection spell to keep tabs on Hamel. I told you I only had enough of the components for one, maybe two castings. I used almost all of them up last night. Maybe I'll be able to cast it again once, but the remaining components are so few the spell won't last more than a handful of minutes. Not long enough unless he's right in front of me, and in the time it takes to cast it..." She shook her head and blew out a frustrated sigh.

Not entirely unexpected, but still the news was less than welcome. But there was no help for it, so Raedrick just nodded and moved over to his own chair, behind his desk.

As he settled onto the strangely-comfortable bare wood of his chair, though, a thought occurred to him.

"Hamel doesn't know that though, does he?"

Melanie blinked. In his chair, Julian perked up a bit.

"And I'm not sure that it really matters," Raedrick said. He leaned back in his chair, feeling its front feet leaving the floor a tad.

"What do you mean?" Julian said.

Raedrick shrugged. "He wasn't wrong. He hasn't caused any trouble at all since he's been here, and honestly I can't blame him if he's using his abilities to coax a town of strangers into liking him more quickly than they otherwise would have."

He could see Julian's face darkening, and Melanie looked at him with an uncertain expression on her face.

"Well what would you have done in his place?" Raedrick asked.

Silence loomed for a moment. Julian's jaw worked and Raedrick expected an explosion of righteous indignation. And rightly so.

But Julian surprised him. He looked away, toward the front door, and let out a long breath that was a cross between a sigh and an aggrieved snort.

"Not bewitch the population, that's for sure." He let out a half-laugh. "But then, I can't do that with anything but my wits and charm."

"And hardly even then," Melanie said.

He looked crossly at her, but she smiled back at him, a mixture of teasing and affection on her face, and Julian rolled his eyes. Then he looked back at Raedrick.

"It's not right, though, what he did."

Raedrick spread his hands and made a little shrug. "If he did it to cause harm, certainly. But he hasn't. At least not yet." He glanced at Melanie. "Have you ever used your magic to gain an advantage, when others didn't know you were doing it?"

She opened her mouth to reply, but stopped. She thought for a moment, then nodded slowly. "Several times." She raised a hand toward Julian as he opened his mouth to retort, and looked seriously at him. "I have, Julian. And not just when you two have asked me to." She inhaled. "It was a long and difficult journey, fleeing the Magestirium. Not knowing if their Inquisitors were on my trail or not, if they were close by to snap me up or not. I had to use every advantage I could, to be able to survive and keep moving."

Julian closed his mouth, and Raedrick could see his jaw working. Obviously Melanie's words had an effect, and he didn't like it. But some of the severity left his face as he considered, and finally, Julian made the smallest of nods. But there was still resistance in his eyes.

"His situation isn't the same as yours was."

Melanie inclined her head in acknowledgment. "No one is chasing him, that's true—"

"That we know of."

Melanie raised an eyebrow at him, and Julian returned it. "Well it's true. We don't know anything about him before he came here."

"Granted. But I think it's more likely he's become accustomed to using his skills in his performances as part of the show. It would encourage tips, if nothing else. It was probably second nature to him, especially when he found himself trapped here for the winter." She looked back at Raedrick. "He probably never even thought about the implications of it."

"But now he has," Raedrick said. "His eyes didn't look as confident as he tried to sound when we left. I think he's going to be more circumspect from now on."

"So, what, we just let him keep on," Julian waved his hand in the air, "spelling the town up each night?"

"No," Raedrick said. "We'll keep an eye on him, like we told him we would." He raised his eyebrows at Melanie. "Is there any way to get more of the components you need between now and spring?"

She shook her head. "No. Two of them are quite rare. My supplier in Mangin City has them in stock, but until the caravans begin coming through again..." She spread her hands helplessly. "I have what I have, and that's it."

"Well then we'll just have to watch him," Raedrick said. "He doesn't know your limitation, so he has to presume we'll catch him if he does it again. So we'll just have to make sure one of us is at each of his performances going forward."

"And since Julian and I have shown ourselves to be more susceptible than the rest of you, we ought to be able to see if he takes advantage again?"

Raedrick nodded. "And now that I know to look for it, I'll bet I can puzzle it out as well."

Julian frowned. "So, deterrence then?"

Melanie nodded, and so did Raedrick. Julian sighed, then nodded after a moment.

"Well, I hear he's playing at Holb's again tonight." He grinned at Raedrick. "You can't go there, so guess I'll have to." The more than half-teasing tone he always used when he broached the dislike between Raedrick and Holb returned, and Raedrick was pleased to see that Julian wasn't going to push back on the plan.

Although…

Raedrick said, "Holb threw you out the other night. Are you sure—?"

Julian waved a dismissive hand. "That's all good. He and I had a laugh about it yesterday."

"That's good, I would hate to see you and Holb stop being bosom buddies."

Melanie chuckled, and Julian grinned broadly at him, and what bit of tension had been in the air just a few moments earlier was gone.

The door to the cell block swung open then and the caravan men tromped through. Jorus came through at the rear and closed the door behind them. He nodded Raedrick's way.

"He didn't say much, Constable. Just mumbled. Thought I heard his brother's name, but I'm not sure."

Raedrick winced. A loss that profound… He didn't think about his brother all that often these days; not much point when he was so far away. But if someone had done to him what Torgens did to Yarnel, and right in front of him?

Julian was right, it was very hard to think of Hab's revenge as anything but justified.

He drew a breath and settled his chair fully back onto the floor, nodding to Jorus. "That's more than he's made for us. Hopefully he's coming out of the spell that's on him."

Across the room, Melanie's eyebrow quirked slightly at his choice of words, but she didn't speak.

Jorus nodded. "The judge decide how to handle him yet?"

Raedrick shook his head. "We filed the report, and he's considering it. If I had to bet I'd say he'll decline to charge and we'll send him back to Master Sebastini's care."

"Sebastini's been checking on him though?"

Raedrick nodded.

Jorus sighed and looked back into the cell block. "Hope you're right, Constable. He didn't do anything but what any man woulda in his place."

That rang close enough to Raedrick's thoughts of a moment ago that he couldn't argue the point.

"Well," Jorus looked at the other caravan men, and they nodded to each other.

"Thanks, Constable," one of them said, and they moved to the front door.

Jorus took up the rear again, but paused just inside the door. He looked over Julian's way. "I hear you saying something about Holb's?"

Julian nodded. "Hamel's playing there tonight."

Jorus perked up, grinning. "It'll be good to see the bard again, and hear 'im. Sebastini wouldn't let me go last night." He shook his foot in the air again. "Wasn't sure the foot was up to it yet. Good to go now, though. Guess I'll see you there."

Julian returned the grin. "Ale's on me, for your trouble."

Jorus poked an index finger at him. "Might make you regret that, Constable." He laughed companionably, then he stepped outside.

The door began to swing shut but stopped as Amos darted within, then pulled it to. He was bundled up in a thick blue wool cloak, lined with grey fur at the neck and emblazoned with the circled M of his family's crest on the breast. He was carrying a lidded cast-iron pot in both hands, and had a pleased expression on his face.

"Got the first meal from the new cooking rotation, Constable," he said, raising the pot in front of himself.

"So that's where you've been," Raedrick replied, putting a small bit of rebuke into his tone.

Amos's face dropped slightly. "I figured no sense in waiting.

Two women have already committed, and two others are thinking it over."

"Fast work," Julian said. He looked, and sounded, almost as pleased as Amos. "Good job. But next time, let us know if you're not going to be here on time. We thought there might be a problem or something."

"Sorry," Amos said, making a subdued shrug beneath the weight of the pot. Then he nodded toward the cell block. "He's awake for a meal?"

"Sure is. And the bucket could use emptying, too," Julian said.

Amos's face fell completely. Then he nodded and headed back into the cell block.

After he left the room, Julian met Raedrick's gaze, and Raedrick couldn't help chuckling. Julian did as well.

LAKESIDE

Julian put his head down and braced himself against a biting wind. It whipped down Lydelton's Main Street like a viper that was seeking his misery above all others. No matter how he turned, it was always blowing straight into his face, shot from an inerrant bow.

In his mind, he knew that was not the case. It was just the buildings lining the street. As the wind whipped from north to south, it funneled down the street and past the buildings, through the gaps between them, so it only seemed to be changing direction.

He knew it, but that did little good against the assault. Pulling his cloak tight, he strode faster, pumping his legs to generate more heat—and get his rounds done more quickly.

It was dark, though the day had barely reached noon. The clouds that had been rolling in yesterday as they left their confrontation with Hamel had thickened and lowered, so now they were a deep grey that made Julian think a thunderstorm was brewing.

This would be worse: a full-on blizzard, and a hard one. He'd seen enough of them last winter here to know the signs. But this was different.

It lingered, the clouds gathering, but not breaking. From the way the overcast had deepened yesterday, he thought the snows would begin before nightfall. But no, just an ominous gathering, like the gods were inhaling before a long, deep blow that would yank the roofs of the Lydelton's structures like they were made of paper.

That was crazy-talk, of course. The houses and buildings of the town were stoutly-built, designed to handle the harsh winters that Glimmer Vale brought. Most roofs were slate; only a few structures, like the ranger station northwest of town, were thatch. And that only because it had been left unused for years.

Still, as Julian turned down the road leading toward the town's finger piers, he couldn't help but shiver, and from more than the cold.

The Covington Brothers's main warehouse filled most of the last stretch of road leading down to the piers, and he noted with satisfaction that they had it secured well, this time. The windows at the front of the building were closed and bolted, the blinds within drawn.

Yesterday, he had found one of the rear windows ajar, to Horace's very vocally-voiced chagrin. He had clearly put a quick stop to that kind of sloppiness.

Not that Julian, or anyone really, expected skulkers or thieving. Not now that winter was setting in and no more caravans would be coming through. But you never knew...

And they did have strangers in town, didn't they? And with whatever Hamel was up to...

He clumped up the rising planks of the pier, barely registering the change in feel from the hard and craggy semi-frozen earth to the smooth, nigh-on slick, wood as he mulled that thought over.

What *was* he up to?

Raedrick was right, Hamel had spoken true. He hadn't actually caused any harm or started any trouble, except in Julian's own head. But he had done that, hadn't he, and they couldn't let him get away with it.

But get away with what, exactly?

Last night's concert had been uneventful. Julian had attended, as planned, and sat through the entire thing. Enjoyed it quite a bit, actually. The bard could sing, he had to admit that. But that was it. Just good music and fun with the rest of the crowd at Holb's tavern.

No weird feelings, no visions—or whatever those had been— no nothing.

So maybe Hamel was cutting it out, now that he knew they were on to him.

And maybe—Julian's stubborn side hated to admit it, but he couldn't throw the idea out completely—Hamel had been telling the entire truth when they confronted him. He really had just been trying to ease his way into a community that he hadn't expected to have to fit into for more than a few days.

Couldn't say he blamed him, if that were really the case. But still, something about it rubbed at Julian the wrong way. He couldn't buy that there was nothing more to it.

He found himself on pier five, the western-most, and slowed as he approached a lone boat, one of only three that still remained tied up on the finger piers. The fishing men had hauled all of the others out of the water to winterize them, to stop them being damaged when the lake inevitably froze over. But the weather had moved in more quickly than they could work, partly because they had extended their fishing season to make up for lost work time earlier in the year.

Now this one, named Betty by the painting on its bow, bobbed and bumped against the bumpers built into the side of the dock while half a dozen men were at work securing its rigging in preparation for the blow about to descend upon the town.

Julian paused beside the boat. After a short while, the oldest of the men, his black hair greying on his temples beneath the wool cap he wore, noticed him and came over to the rail closest the pier.

"Constable," he said, nodding in greeting. Julian recognized him, of course. Ken was ten or fifteen years Julian's senior and well-respected among the fishing men, having risen to captaining the Betty almost by popular acclaim.

"I figured you fellows would be indoors where it's warm by now," Julian said, and Ken snorted.

"I could say the same about you." He breathed out a misting breath and looked over his shoulder, to where his men were working at folding up a big bundle of grey canvas—the boat's mainsail or Julian was a rooster. "Soon as this blows through," he gestured toward the sky to the north, "we're hauling her out. No time to waste once she's ashore, so we gotta get as much done now as we can."

Julian looked up at the looming cloud cover, then over at the shore, where he could see other men working on the apparatus that the fishing men used to haul their boats out. Several were readying the lines that would be used to pull on the boat, while others were arranging the boards that would support and guide the boat up into the cradle that would support its weight for the winter.

The rest of the fleet was already laid out there, and other men were busy tying down tarps atop the more recently-hauled boats.

A big job, all around.

He nodded toward the workers ashore. "Looks like they're almost ready to go. You don't think there'll be time to get her out before it starts?"

Ken shook his head with a snort. "Spray and Tempest go ahead of us." He indicated the other two remaining boats that were tied to the docks.

Looking over at them, Julian could see that their crews were hard at work as well.

"Luck of the draw," Ken continued. "We were last out this year, so last in as well." He waggled his eyebrows at Julian. "That way no one can say some crews put in less time than others."

"I suppose that makes sense."

Ken nodded. "Horace's idea, a few years back. It solved some squabbling over pay. Anyway, it'll take all afternoon to get Spray out and secured. Gotta pull down the mast, and can't do that without the gantry over there. That means Tempest and us wait til after the blow."

Julian supposed that made sense. He looked back over Betty, and her crew. "You need anything?"

Ken grinned at him. "You got some warm weather to hand out, Constable?"

Chuckling, Julian shook his head. He clasped hands with Ken and bid him and his men farewell, then turned and walked back toward shore.

He spied another figure departing from Tempest, who was tied at pier three. He was bundled up in a blue cloak with the cowl thrown up, and he had a bundle of some sort on his back. As Julian drew nearer, he saw golden locks blowing out one side of the cowl, and he realized that wasn't a bundle; it was a harp case.

Julian slowed as Hamel noticed him. They met where pier three met up at the cross-planks that joined the heads of all the finger piers, connecting them with the main walkway back to shore.

"Good day, Constable," the bard said, and his tone was cheerful, apparently unguarded, without a concern in the world.

"Hamel," Julian said. Gesturing toward the cased instrument, he said, "The boat crew wanted some music?"

Hamel let out a little laugh and shook his head. "I dare say it might lighten their burden a bit. But no, your former mayor asked me to come by to play for his wife this afternoon. Her health is failing, or so I hear. I didn't want to have to go back to my rooms for it, so I brought my harp with me on the morning's excursions."

Julian frowned, wincing inwardly. Raedrick had told him the reason why Mayor Brimly had decided not to stand for re-election, but even if he hadn't, it was no longer much of a secret around town. The rumor-mill said she had only months left, and she hadn't left their house in weeks.

Sad, that. He hadn't spent a whole lot of time with Mistress Brimly, but she had always been cheerful and pleasant, a fine balance against her husband's tendency toward grumpiness.

"That's good of you," he said.

"Least I can do in return for the hospitality your town has shown me."

Julian wasn't sure if there was a jab in there, over the previous day's confrontation. Hamel's tone certainly didn't show it, nor did his expression, open and honest as the day was long.

Of course, the days weren't all that long right now, and getting shorter by the week.

"Wish her well for me."

Hamel nodded. "I shall."

Julian turned to go, but Hamel moved to walk with him. As they walked down the sloping planks that led down to the shore, the bard cleared his throat and looked sidelong at him.

"I spoke with Jorus last night after the show."

"Is that right."

Hamel nodded. "He told me what happened with Hab and his brother. I understand Hab is in one of your holding cells?"

"Yes. Why?"

"I was with the caravan for several weeks, and became friendly with him and his brother." Hamel paused, and looked sidelong at Julian again. "I'd like to visit with him, if I could."

That was unexpected. Julian had seen him honor the caravan men at his concert two nights ago, and spend time engaging with Jorus last night. But he'd presumed it was from politeness, the better to appeal to the crowd.

But on Hamel's face now was genuine concern, or at least he was putting on such a good show of it that he should have been a con artist, not a musician.

Well, being tricksy with magic didn't mean he couldn't genuinely make friends, Julian supposed.

"He's not really all there, you know."

Hamel nodded.

"Jorus and the others came by yesterday, and it seemed to do him some good. If you really were friends, maybe it'll help more."

Hamel's lips compressed slightly at that little barb, but he didn't reply. Julian nodded to himself.

"I'm about done with my rounds. Assuming you're not going to spell him up," he gave Hamel a hard look, "I'll let you in once we get to the Constabulary."

Hamel laughed, shaking his head. "Constable, even if I had the ability to, as you say, spell him up, I could hardly do it with you watching my every move, could I?"

Julian grunted, and his boot struck the hardened earth of the shore. "Come on then," he said.

The walk from the finger piers to the Constabulary normally only took a few short minutes. But this time, between the wind seeming to pick up from one moment to the next and the uncomfortable silence between him and Hamel, it felt to Julian like it took an hour.

But finally, they turned from Main Street and he saw the building up ahead on the left.

"You been in a jail before?" Julian said.

Hamel nodded.

Julian chuckled. Of course he had. "Same rules here. Don't pass anything through the bars, and don't—"

A woman's scream rang out, and Julian froze.

Ahead, the door to the Constabulary burst open and a figure darted out, and then jumped down the three stairs from the porch down to the street.

The figure was not bundled for the cold, just wearing leggings, boots, and a tunic. He looked right and saw Julian and Hamel, then immediately turned and ran off down the street.

"What the—?" Hamel said.

"Was that—?" Julian said, at the same time.

Because it looked like Hab. But that couldn't be right.

The woman screamed again, and Julian surged forward. He was to the Constabulary building, up the stairs, and through the front door in a heartbeat.

The front office was toasty warm, but Julian hardly noticed. There was a woman sprawled on the floor, face-down, before Raedrick's desk. Her dress was torn at the hem and her hair, which had once been blond but was now mostly silver, had been neatly braided, but now was pulled askew and disheveled.

Past her, the cell block door was open, and Julian could see clearly beyond into the cell block.

Amos was lying on the floor opposite the door to Hab's cell. A cast iron pot was upturned next to him, its contents spilled out so that he was half-lying in a pool of broth, meats, and vegetables of some kind.

And Hab's cell door was wide open.

"Son of a bitch!" Julian said.

The woman boosted herself up onto her hands and knees, and turned her head toward Julian. He recognized her: it was Ilsa, the wife of Baelin the woodsman, who had been killed by the Out-Dweller a year and a half ago.

She had found work after her husband died, but Julian knew times had been hard for her and her kids, regardless. Not at all surprising she would have jumped at Amos's idea.

"What happened here?" Hamel said, from just inside the doorway.

"Check on him," Julian said, pointing at Amos, then he took a knee next to Ilsa. "Are you alright?"

He heard Hamel moving past him toward the cell block, and felt a flash of surprise that the bard just did it. But he put that out of his mind, focusing in on Ilsa as she drew a deep breath, then nodded.

"He…he just came out like an animal, Julian. Amos opened the cell to give him lunch, and…" Her voice caught in her throat and she shook her head.

She moved to straighten up, and Julian stood, offering her a hand. She accepted it with a grateful look, then boosted herself to her feet. She swayed slightly, and pressed her hand to her temple, but after a moment, she visibly steeled herself and came to her full height.

"He threw Amos against the bars, and grabbed me by my hair. I thought he would—" She stopped, swallowed. Then she lifted her chin. "But he just shoved me down. I hit the desk and fell. And then he was gone."

"Dammit," Julian said. He looked toward the cell block. "Hamel?"

The bard was crouched over Amos. He had his fingers on the side of the young man's throat, feeling for his pulse. After a moment, he nodded and straightened, meeting Julian's gaze.

"He's alive. Just knocked out; looks like he hit his head against the bars here."

"Ok." He looked back at Ilsa. "Can you walk?"

She nodded.

"Go get Master Sebastini and bring him here to see to Amos." He turned toward the door. "Hamel," he said, not bothering to look back at him, "get Raedrick. He should be at his house for lunch."

"What are you going to do?"

"I'm getting Hab."

Then he was out the door and onto the street. He turned left, and charged off in the direction Hab had run.

❦ 23 ❦
PURSUIT

It was awkward running down the street, with the unevenly-packed dirt all but frozen through, patches of ice hither and yon, and, once Julian turned onto a crossing street, a whole lot of residual snow to blunder through.

Apparently the street clearing crews hadn't made it everywhere, yet.

He slowed immediately as he stepped into a calf-deep snowdrift, and he glowered for moment. He hated wading through snow.

But the weather would impede Hab all the more, without layers, cloak, gloves, and hat. He wouldn't be able to get very far before he'd either have to find a place to stop or just collapse from exposure.

Julian needed to catch him before either of those things happen.

He killed a man; maybe succumbing to exposure would be his just deserts.

Julian shoved that thought down, hard. What Hab had done wasn't murder, not by any measure. The judge hadn't fully decided it yet, but Julian was certain that was where he'd come down.

But even if the judge didn't, Julian and Raedrick had sworn to uphold the law, and that meant Hab would get his day in court to see what justice truly required.

So yes, Julian needed to catch him. Quickly.

But where had he gone?

Hab had been running quickly, but Julian hadn't spent all that long in the Constabulary before giving chase. Especially in these conditions, he couldn't have—

A crash, then the sound of wood splintering from ahead and to the right brought Julian out of his reverie. The wind was blowing into his face, making his cheeks burn from cold, and he found himself squinting against the force of it. But he was pretty sure the sound came from a two-story house up ahead, just before the next intersection.

The building was capped by a peaked, steeply-sloping roof, like almost all of the buildings in Lydelton. It looked to be the type that had a larger living space on the first floor and a smaller flat on the second. Julian could see the stairs leading up to that flat, mounted on the side of the building facing him, and open to the elements.

And was the door to that flat hanging ajar?

Julian hurried to the staircase and charged up two at a time. Halfway up, he could see that, yes, the door was hanging open; in fact the door's frame was visibly cracked, like the door had been kicked in.

"Got you," he said as he neared the top of the stairs.

Then a man's angry voice, shouting, "Get out of here!" came through the broken door, and Hab stumbled back onto the landing. His left hand was pressed to his nose, and blood was trickling down his chin.

The flat's owner must have punched him something good.

"Stop, Hab," Julian commanded. He was three steps from the landing, and considered pulling his short sword. Just as quickly, he discarded the thought.

Hab was out of sorts from the shock of his experience, probably not really looking to hurt anyone. And he was unarmed.

Hab turned toward Julian as his words rang out, and for a second he froze. Then he dropped his left hand to his side, revealing a blood-smeared face and flattened nose. And wide, wild, eyes that darted from Julian to the ground behind and below him, to the door he had just stumbled through, and back.

He looked feral, wild.

Julian was just beginning to think he was mistaken about not drawing steel when Hab uttered an incoherent, growling shout and charged him.

Julian was a bit taller than him, and had more muscle. But that advantage disappeared against Hab's higher position, and he found himself borne down by the man's weight suddenly smashing into him. He tottered for a second, then the world went upside down as he fell.

The wood of the stairs smacked his shoulder, then his hip, and then he was rolling, twisted up with Hab's body as they both tumbled down the stairs.

At some point, Julian's head smacked something hard and he saw stars. Pain flared from his skull and his tongue both as he reflexively bit down from the impact. The metallic flavor of blood filled his mouth.

Again he rolled, and his knee racked itself on a stair.

Then he struck the frozen dirt and rolled onto his back, his head still spinning and only able to think of the new aches and pains, apparently all over his body. He heard himself groaning, but it was like someone else doing it.

Vaguely, somewhere off to his left, he heard scrabbling movement. Someone rushing to push himself to his feet?

Julian needed to get moving, stop whoever it was from doing...something. But right then the thought of who, what, and why didn't come to him through the aching haze that filled his head, like the dark grey that filled his vision.

He shook his head and blinked his eyes but the grey remained.

Then a shape moved into sight, different from the grey, and everything snapped back into focus.

He had been looking at the overcast clouds, and now Hab was standing over him, looking down at him with his bloody face and feral gaze. The wild man tensed, and Julian moved by instinct, rolling to his right.

His shoulder screamed out in protest at the roll, but the heavy thump against the dirt he had just vacated silenced its shout.

That boot to the head would have hurt a lot more, and maybe worse.

Julian rolled to his belly and pushed himself up onto his hands and knees, and saw Hab moving toward him again, foot pulling back for another kick.

He pushed himself backward, and he landed on his backside. Hab's kick passed harmlessly in front of him, but he was going to come again, Julian was certain of that. The wildness in his eyes hadn't let up; if anything it had become worse.

Julian's hand found the grip of his short sword and he began to draw it.

A shout from above, and the sound of heavy booted feet on wood, drew Hab's gaze away from Julian, and the wild man's eyes widened. He swallowed and took a hesitant step backwards. Then he licked his lips and turned away, running in a zig-zagging gait, the kind a drunk man might make, that nevertheless ate up distance quickly.

He vanished around the left-hand turn at the next intersection.

"You alright, Constable?" said the man who was descending the staircase. The fellow who had punched Hab upstairs and now had saved Julian's hide.

He was half a head taller than Julian, and burly, with a dark brown beard that flowed down to his collar and a fully-shaved crown. He wore yellow-white shirtsleeves and loose, dark brown leggings that were tucked into his boots, and a deep scowl of affront as he bounded to Julian's side.

Julian recognized him: Barran, one of the woodcutters who

ventured into the Glamorwood during the warm months, and in the winter helped to keep the streets clear.

"Think so," Julian said, and moved to stand. But his left knee protested and he stopped with a grimace.

Barran offered him a hand up, and Julian accepted it.

"Thanks." After he got to his feet, Julian tested his knee by shifting his weight, and the initial protest was less, but still there.

Wonderful.

He nodded up at Barran's flat. "How about you?"

Barran's scowl deepened. "I was in the back room, helping Candace give little William a bath, when he burst in." He saw the question before Julian could voice it, and shook his head. "They're fine. Just frightened."

He looked down the street in the direction Hab had disappeared. "What's he on about?"

"It's a long story." Julian tugged at his cloak to get it hanging right, and grimaced as his right shoulder sang out against the movement. "I'd better be after him, before he does something worse." He clapped Barran on the arm. "Thanks again."

But when he turned to go, his knee flared up again, and he stumbled a step before he could right himself.

"You don't look up for a chase, you don't mind my saying," Barran said.

And he was probably right. Julian's knee and shoulder both ached, his head was pounding, and he still tasted blood. But… He put on what he hoped was a reassuring grin and said, "Yeah, well, it's my job."

Julian limped away, taking it easy at first, but after a few steps he found he was able to increase the pace a bit, and by the time he rounded the corner where Hab had disappeared he almost could manage a slow trot.

Almost.

He looked down the street toward the lake, four blocks down. There were not very many people out and about, and all were scrunched up in their cloaks against the cold and the wind. But two people immediately stood out, down by the intersection with Main Street's paving stones. The one was helping the other to his feet, and staring to the right, down Main Street toward the Town Hall. It was far enough away that Julian couldn't make out expressions, but the fellow's angry look was obvious nonetheless.

No mystery which way Hab went.

His knee felt a little bit better by the time he reached the two fellows, but he still felt it with every step. So the scowl he was wearing when he stopped next to them was from annoyance and hurt as much as anything else.

They took a step back from him, though. The man who had regained his feet pointed down the street. "He went that way, ducked down toward the fish warehouse."

Julian nodded, and hurried as best he could.

A few steps later, he heard boots on the stones behind him, and Barran slowed to match his pace on his right. He had donned a thick, fur-lined brown cloak, and he clutched a stout wooden cudgel in his right hand.

He glanced Julian's way. "You need help."

Julian felt a protest welling up, but stomped down on it. Raedrick would be on his way, but who knew how long it would take him to find them. In the meantime… He did need help.

Julian nodded. "Come on."

✣ 24 ✣

RENDEZVOUS

Raedrick was still tugging his sword belt tight about his waist as he pushed through his door and out onto Main Street. He paused just a heartbeat to look left and right before turning to run toward the Constabulary.

Hamel followed behind him and to his left, puffing a bit as he hurried to keep up. Apparently physical exertion wasn't something Hamel was very acquainted with. It would have been amusing at another time.

Raedrick slowed a bit, and Hamel drew up next to him with a grateful look.

The distance from his flat to the Constabulary passed quickly enough, but it felt a relative eternity. The door was open, and Raedrick took a moment to look inside. There was no one in there, but he saw a woman and a man in the Healers Circle's colors approaching from down the street.

Ilsa, returning with Sebastini. No, the guildsman was moving too quickly. Must be Willam.

"Did you see where he went?" Raedrick asked Hamel

The bard was bent forward a bit, his hands on his thighs as he was catching his breath. "Away from the lake and to the left," the bard said, his voice breaking a bit in between breaths.

Raedrick looked that direction, frowning, and thought about the town's layout. If Hab went that way, he'd reach the last of the town's buildings quickly, and he'd either have to turn around or continue on into the wilderness.

But there was already a fair amount of snow of the ground, and little shelter or warmth to be found, not in Hab's state. Not likely he'd flee into the hills, even if he was out of his mind.

Raedrick nodded to himself and turned back toward Main Street.

Hamel blinked in surprise, and pointed the other way. "Constable—"

"Come on, if you're coming," Raedrick said, and charged off.

Back on the paved street, he turned right, toward the Town Hall, and picked up the pace, his mind churning through the most likely places Hab might go to. Holb's Tavern was only a few blocks away, with not much more than canvas for walls and plenty of warmth within. But also a fair number of people, even at this hour of the day.

Bigsbe's Boarding House, maybe? There were lots of rooms that he might be able to slip into if he managed to get past the attendant on duty.

Or maybe—

"There," Hamel said, and pointed down the street ahead of them.

Raedrick squinted into the wind blowing in his face, and immediately saw what the bard was pointing at.

Two men, veering off Main Street toward the Covington Brothers's buildings, both cloaked. But one had what looked like a club in his hands, and Raedrick saw a scabbarded short sword on the other's hip.

Julian, and one of the men from the town, who had apparently joined in the chase.

Raedrick nodded. "Hurry."

He sped up even more, and Hamel fell behind, but this time Raedrick didn't slow for him. Raedrick needed to link up with

Julian, and the sooner the better. The bard would just have to catch up if he wanted to assist.

It occurred to him that it was odd that Hamel would do that, considering the accusation he and Julian had leveled against him the other day. Or then again, maybe not. If he really had been on the up and up, Hamel would want to assure him and Julian that he meant well.

Or even if he wasn't, said that suspicious side of Raedrick's mind.

But that was a thought for another time, and he set it aside as he rounded the corner and saw Julian and the unknown man stopped at the front door of the Covington Brothers's warehouse.

The door was flung wide open, the darkened interior of the building beckoning, but also sending a warning against anyone thinking to enter. Right then, the dim light of the overcast day seemed bright as noon compared with the gloom past that entryway.

Raedrick shook that bit of oddness from his mind, and called out, "Julian!"

Julian stopped in mid-step, as he had begun to ascend the steps leading up to the open door. Seeing Raedrick, he waved for him to approach.

"Hab's in there," Julian said as Raedrick drew to a halt beside him and the large, bald and bearded fellow with him. He was familiar, of course, but right that moment Raedrick couldn't place his name.

Raedrick nodded and peered into the darkness past the doorway. "Do you—?" He stopped as Julian's appearance fully registered, and took a hard look at him.

He looked like hell. There was a large welt, turning into a larger bruise, on the right side of his forehead, and blood was trickling out of the side of his mouth. And he was obviously favoring his left leg.

"What happened to you?"

The bearded man piped up, "The madman tackled him down a flight of stairs."

Raedrick wasn't sure how to respond to that for a second.

Julian shrugged, his left shoulder rising more than his right. "I'm alright," he said.

Raedrick wasn't so sure about that. "You don't look it. Why don't you stay here and guard the door with Hamel and," he gestured toward the bearded man, "we'll go in after him." To be sure, though, he glanced over his shoulder and yes, the bard was making up the distance quickly to join them.

Julian opened his mouth to protest, and a larger trickle of blood leaked out. He must have felt it, because he grimaced and wiped his mouth with the back of his hand, then spat out a mouthful of red onto the ground. Then, with reluctance, he nodded.

"Be careful, Rae," Julian said. "Hab's gone wild. I'm not sure he wouldn't have kicked me to death if Barran hadn't chased him off."

The bearded man—Barran—looked almost embarrassed at Julian's words. Inwardly, Raedrick thanked Julian for the reminder of his name.

He looked Barran up and down. He was certainly sturdy, and from the way he carried that club it appeared he knew how to use it. "Are you ready?"

Barran nodded, his face turning grimly resolved.

Hamel pulled up then, panting and red-faced from exertion. He rolled his shoulders, and the big harp case on his back shifted.

"Stay here with Julian," Raedrick said to the bard. "Be ready if we need help." Then he nodded to Barran. "Let's go."

25

THE WILDEST OF BEASTS

The interior was less dark than it had appeared from outside, but it was still dim. The lamps within the warehouse were extinguished; even the office at the other end of the front room was dark.

No surprise about that. At this point, all of the fishing men were focused on winterizing their boats, and until the town needed to start drawing on the winter stockpiles, besides his and Julian's periodic checks, there wasn't much reason for anyone to come in here.

Still, it seemed oppressively empty, ominously silent as Raedrick entered, Barran at his heels.

He squinted against the dimness as his eyes adjusted, hunting the shadows for anything that was out of place from when he'd last been in here two days before.

Nothing. All seemed just as it had been.

"You're sure he's in here?" he said quietly.

Barran grunted. "He barreled past a group of kids on their way home from Helena's school. They saw him come in, plain as day."

Raedrick nodded, frowning.

Why would Hab have come in here? Was it just mad flight, or

was there a purpose to it? He couldn't think of what that purpose might be; there wasn't much in here that would be of use to him.

But then, Hab didn't know that, did he?

"Check the office," he said, gesturing toward its open door-way. "I'll look in the store room."

Barran looked uncertain for a moment, then he nodded, and began making his way slowly, and much more quietly than Raedrick would have thought a man of his size could manage.

The fish stores were frozen, but despite that, its odor grew intense as Raedrick ducked his head through the doorway into the store room. The window coverings were pulled to, in anticipation of the coming storm, so the room was even more dim. But he could make out the familiar shapes of the storage bins and the lumpy masses of preserved fish beneath piled up ice shavings and packed snow.

Nothing seemed out of place, and nothing moved in the gloom.

The furtive sounds of Barran's movement from the front room were the only sounds aside from the faint howling of wind past the raised eaves of the building's exterior.

He slipped further inside, straining to see, to hear. But there was nothing.

Where was Hab?"

Raedrick decided to risk calling out. "Hab?" he said into the gloom. "Come out. We're here to help you."

His voice seemed to echo, but there was no reply. No hint of movement.

Had he climbed up into the rafters, perhaps?

Raedrick lifted his head, peering at the thick beams that criss-crossed above him, supporting the structure's peaked roof. It was so dark up there a dozen men could be crouching and he wouldn't be able to find them.

They would need to get the lamps lit, or bring in torches, to really check up there. And he hadn't brought flint and steel, just his cloak and sword.

"Dammit," he said softly, and he turned to go back into the front room.

He paused, though, when a movement, a shadow atop a shadow back in the rear right-hand corner that was so subtle he almost missed it, caught his eye.

Raedrick focused in on the corner, willing greater light to come from somewhere. And for a moment he thought maybe, somehow, some had, because it seemed he could see things back there more clearly. He imagined he could see the seam where the two walls met, the nails holding the interior siding in place.

But then the moment faded like it had never been, and he decided he was just imposing his memory of the room onto what he was seeing. His eyes were playing tricks on him, and no wonder considering the—

The motion returned, down near the floor, and this time he was certain he wasn't imagining it.

It was low, moving steadily along the wall toward him. Too low for a man standing, but not for one crouched down, or crawling…

He moved forward, stepping closer to the storage bins to give the whatever-it-was a wide berth. If it was Hab, trying to sneak his way out, better to let him think Raedrick hadn't seen him.

So Raedrick kept his body and head straight, not turning to look at the pocket of motion except from the corner of his eye.

It was continuing along the wall, toward the door Raedrick had just abandoned, and a grim assurance, that this was in fact Hab, began to grow within him. He fingered the hilt of his sword with the fingers of his left hand, the leather wrapping on its grip reassuring in its tactile familiarity.

He didn't want to have to use the weapon; far from it. But Hab had already badly injured Julian, and—

A loud crashing from out in the front room broke Raedrick's chain of thought.

"Constable!" reached his ears—a shout from Barran—at the same time a squeak came from over by the wall, and the bit of motion Raedrick had been watching shifted and retreated, becoming lost in the darkness almost as soon as it changed direction.

Had he been chasing a rat?

Barran shouted again, and another crash rang out, and Raedrick was to the doorway back to the front room in a flash.

He burst through and saw Barran, a smaller man clinging to his back with his legs entwined among Barran's and one arm wrapped around his neck. The other arm was bent toward the big man's chest, and even in the dim light Raedrick could see the gleam of metal clenched in Hab's hand.

Barran's eyes were wide, and he had both hands up, clenched around Hab's forearm to keep the knife from impaling him.

Raedrick watched, aghast, as the entwined pair spun a circle in the center of the room. Then Barran overbalanced, and the two of them stumbled over to the side, where a bunch of crates were stacked.

The big man collided with one of the crates side-on. The force of the impact made him stumble further, and his hands slipped from Hab's forearm.

"Hab, no!" Raedrick shouted as he sprang forward, hoping against hope that he could get there in time.

He half-heard Julian's voice from behind him, and footsteps as he came inside to help.

Time seemed to slow to a deadly crawl. The knife plunged toward Barran's chest. There was nothing that could stop it.

But the big man was also moving, rebounding off the crate and falling forward, Hab's weight on his back helping him along.

Plunging knife and falling body merged into a confusion of limbs as the pair of them struck the ground.

Barran cried out, and Hab rolled over the top of him, landing on his back with his feet facing Raedrick and his head a foot or so away from Barran's.

Everything was still for a small eternity, then Barran cried out again and rolled to his left, onto his back. His left hand went to a deep gash in the meat of his right shoulder, and Raedrick could see a blood trail on the floor from where he had lain.

Hab moved as well, rolling up into a crouch. He still had the knife, and it was dripping dark fluid off its blade. From this distance, Raedrick could see it was a scaling knife, meant for use on the day's catch.

But it would work just fine on a man.

Barran shoved himself away from the wild man, pushed with the heels of his boots against the floor to put distance between himself and Hab. His club lay on the floor over by the office door, but from the way he was clutching at his wound, Raedrick was sure he wouldn't be able to use it effectively. Not with his right arm, anyway.

But Hab wasn't paying Barran any mind. His eyes, narrowed to slits, were fixed on Raedrick, and he ran his tongue across his lips.

In the dim light, the sclera of his eyes, what little was visible, seemed to glow.

Raedrick got the impression of a wild beast, a hunting predator, preparing to spring on its prey, and he got a chill down his spine.

His right hand found the grip of his sword, and he tensed to pull the length of steel, honed to beyond a razor's edge.

To his left, he saw Julian, short sword drawn, moving as smoothly as his injured leg would allow.

Hab saw him as well, and his eyes darted from Raedrick to Julian and back again. He sank into a lower crouch, and Raedrick could feel him tensing.

Raedrick held out his left hand toward Hab, palm open. He opened his mouth to order Hab to stand down.

But Hamel's voice rang through the room before he could say anything, and Raedrick found he could not speak at all in place of it.

"Do you remember me, Hab?"

He was speaking, not singing, but it felt like the words themselves were wound through with every note of music ever invented. And somehow, a few that had never been voiced before.

Hab's demeanor shifted. The tension, the readiness to spring, remained, but he stilled, looking away from Raedrick to the space behind him and to his left.

Raedrick followed his gaze and saw Hamel, unlimbering his harp case from where it had been strapped to his back as he strode slowly forward toward a table set against the wall.

"Be at peace, my friend," Hamel said, his words drawing out now so that they were approaching song.

Hab moved, slowly, in Hamel's direction. His fingers flexed on the grip of the knife, and his eyes blinked rapidly, and Raedrick thought he was going to spring.

Then the bard sat up on the table's edge and positioned his harp, and his fingers ran across the strings.

Melody flowed forth, then repeated along with a counter-melody that spoke of peace and safety, of calm and rest. It continued, and at some point Hamel began truly singing.

The words were lost on Raedrick; he only registered the feeling they conveyed.

Peace. Peace and Calm.

Rest and safety.

Comfort.

He lost track of the passage of time, caught up in the flow of the song, and he noticed absently that he had relaxed his grip on his sword; his left arm had lowered to his side.

Julian, too, had stopped, lowering his blade and breathing easily. On the far side of Hab, Barran almost seemed to be resting at ease, despite the blood flowing from the wound in his shoulder.

But was that flow reducing as well?

This was dangerous. They were all lowering their guard. If Hab decided to attack...

But the wild man merely stood, transfixed. He straightened noticeably, and his blinking grew more slow. The feral scowl on his face remained, but the tension went out of his shoulders and arms.

The song flowed on, reaching a crescendo of soothing warmth, and Hab's arms dropped to his sides.

He began to tremble all over. His eyes rolled up toward the rafters, and that trembling seemed to coalesce on his face. The scowl seemed to fight against itself, as if it was willing the wild man to never give it up.

A final chord progression came from the harp, then there was just a long, low note carried by Hamel's voice. It went on and on, for a seeming eternity, then slowly faded into deep silence.

The silence lingered until it was broken by a metallic tinkling as the knife fell from Hab's hand.

Then Hab himself collapsed to the floor. He curled up into a ball on his side, hugging his knees to his chest and rocking back and forth, as sobs, sobs carrying loss and despair but also somehow a hint of the promise of healing to come, issued from him.

They all just stared at Hab for a moment, then as one Raedrick, Julian, and Barran looked at Hamel. From their expressions, Julian and Barran were just as moved, and just as perplexed by it, as Raedrick felt.

Hamel shrugged, and smiled a little knowing smile at them.

"Music can soothe even the wildest of beasts," he said.

26

DEBRIEFING

Mayor Holliman sat behind his desk with his shirtsleeves rolled up to just below his elbows. He was in blue today, and somehow managed to look more formally in control than Brimly ever had in his finest coat.

But maybe that was just because Julian still wasn't used to him being there instead of Brimly.

Julian hurt all over. His arm was in a sling, and he wore a brace on his knee. A brace that Sebastini had told him in no uncertain terms he was not to take off—not even in bed—for a month, except to change clothes and bathe. But from his expression, Julian had the impression he would have been happier if Julian didn't bother with either of those during that whole time.

Uncomfortable as those were, though, the ache in his head was the worst. Even now, the morning after the fight with Hab, it throbbed, and he sometimes felt a bit dizzy, bordering on nauseous. Sebastini said that would heal much sooner than his knee and shoulder, but right then he doubted it.

He stood before the mayor's desk next to Raedrick. Sebastini was there as well, seated in one of the mayor's guest chairs, and the judge as well. He was not in his formal robes—this wasn't an actual hearing—but in an everyday coat of red-dyed wool and black leggings that fell loosely around the top of his boots.

"Are you certain about your diagnosis, Guildmaster?" the judge asked.

Sebastini shrugged, the white and yellow robes of his order swishing softly with the movement. "Only time will tell. Perhaps Hab's mind will return to him, but for the foreseeable future, he hardly registers where he is and what is happening around him. Whatever set him off, and whatever broke him from the spell of madness that was on him, it left him completely detached."

"Is there no way to treat it?" Holliman asked, and Sebastini shrugged again.

"Time is all, Master Mayor. There are potions I can give him, but they have never been shown to be fully effective on their own. Until his mind heals itself—if it ever does—all I can do for certain is keep him alive and comfortable."

The mayor and the judge traded glances.

After a moment, the judge sighed. "I cannot try a man in that state, Master Mayor."

Holliman nodded and looked back at Raedrick and Julian. "In that case, there's nothing for it. You'll have to keep him locked up until he's well enough for trial. I'm not willing to risk another incident with him," Holliman said, echoing Julian's own unspoken thought.

Beside him, Raedrick nodded agreement, but he looked troubled. "We don't usually have a lot of trouble in the winter, but once the caravans start again we may need the space. And anyway, I don't think we should keep him locked up here forever."

Sebastini said, "Our order has a Sanitarium in Harrowhold. I suggest we transfer him there in the Spring."

Julian pursed his lips. Harrowhold was about halfway between Mangin City and the Capital, at least a month and a half's journey, one way. Not a fun trip, and certainly not one that he and Raedrick could make. He looked at Raedrick and saw that he was thinking the same thing.

Raedrick said, "I'll send a pigeon to the Royal Marshals after the storm passes." As if hearing itself mentioned, that storm—which had begun dumping its snow on the town last night—produced an extra gust of wind that whistled shrilly past the office's large windows.

Everyone's eyes turned toward the windows for a moment, despite the fact that the view was almost completely obscured by large snowflakes being driven on the wind. Julian could barely make out the buildings on the other side of Main Street.

Clearing his throat, Raedrick continued, "I'll ask them to be prepared to transport him when they come up next."

Holliman said, "Agreed." He sighed and shook his head, clasping his hands in front of himself on the desk. "What about young Melton?"

Sebastini spoke up. "A blow to the head and a few bruises, but he's young. He's already up and about, and eager to be back to work."

"Good." Holliman looked at Julian and made a rueful grin. "I guess you got the worst of it, didn't you? Sorry to welcome you back home so roughly."

"All part of the job," Julian replied, and the Mayor chuckled.

"Not part of Barran's though," Raedrick said. "Once he's recovered, I think a commendation from your office would be appropriate, Master Mayor."

"I've already got the clerk writing one up," Holliman said. "And for Hamel as well." His eyebrows rose. "I daresay he'll not have to buy as drink for the rest of his time here. Who would have thought a song could have such an effect on a madman?" He shook his head. "Amazing."

Julian felt an urge to speak up, to correct the mayor's assumptions. But his and Raedrick's earlier discussion about that subject stopped him. Instead he just nodded agreement.

Mayor Holliman remained silent for a time, obviously

thinking things through. He looked to Sebastini, then the judge, and raised his eyebrows. Both shook their heads; they had nothing more to add. So Holliman nodded and said, "Thank you, gentlemen."

The dismissal was plain, and Julian wasted no time in following Raedrick out of the office.

Descending the stairs to the ground floor was awkward with his braced knee, and Julian winced each step down. While he made his slow way down, Raedrick took his cloak off one of the pegs by the door and donned it, then grabbed Julian's. He helped Julian get the cloak on, clasped, and wrapped tightly about his body, then they stepped outside.

The wind-driven snow was an immediate blow, and Julian scrunched up, trying in vain to draw his cloak even tighter. Raedrick did the same, but he also tapped the brooch that Melanie had given him, and the telltale flash of red from it said the warming enchantment was active.

"Remind me to get Melanie to make me one of those," he said, and Raedrick grinned at him.

"She didn't tell me exactly how much it cost to do, but it wasn't cheap. But then again, you've got plenty of coin to afford it now."

"Yeah."

They descended the steps to Main Street and turned left. As soon as they were away from the building, Julian leaned in closer to Raedrick and spoke quietly. Although there weren't any people around and the wind would make it hard to hear past a few feet, he didn't want his voice to carry.

"Are you sure we shouldn't tell the Mayor about Hamel's...tricks?"

Raedrick frowned. "He seemed very keen on not having it be known, even after we told him we knew about it."

"He was quick enough to threaten spilling *our* secrets."

"True. But he didn't have to help, yesterday. And if he hadn't, more blood would have been spilled."

Julian couldn't deny that. But he still didn't entirely trust the bard. He let it drop, though. They'd discussed this already, last night after they finished cleaning up the immediate effects of Hab's flight and seen him secured again.

Now, they passed the street leading to the Constabulary on their left and continued on. A few long minutes of walking, and getting more chilled by the second, the bulk of The Oarlock appeared out of the whiteout ahead, and they veered toward it.

"You told Melanie to meet us here, yes?"

Julian nodded. "She seemed eager for a rematch."

Raedrick made a half-snort, half laughing sound, and they turned into the inn's stableyard. "Let's hope it doesn't come to that."

27

MORNING TEA

Hamel's smile of welcome when he opened the door to his suite and gestured for them to enter appeared entirely genuine, without guile at all. But there was a shadow in his eyes that, to Julian, spoke of apprehension.

He supposed he couldn't blame the bard for that. But it didn't help him shake the distrust that still lingered.

"I expected you'd come by again," Hamel said as he took a seat in one of the two chairs across from the couch. He gestured toward the short table, where he had a teapot and four cups laid out. The pot was still leaking a bit of steam from its spout; he must have just finished having it heated.

Could he do that with his music magic? Julian had no idea, but it made him a little nervous, to be honest. That was much more… direct…than anything Hamel had done so far. And if he could…

But then again, the stove in the corner of the room was lit and well-fueled, so no need to jump to that sort of conclusion. Yet.

He sat next to Melanie on the couch, and Raedrick took the other chair. This time, Julian waited for Raedrick to start.

He leaned forward, resting his elbows on his knees, and fixed Hamel with a direct, no-nonsense stare. "After what happened yesterday, I think it's time we drop the act," he said, in a tone to match his gaze.

Hamel nodded slowly. "I suppose it is." He bent forward and picked up the teapot. He filled all four cups, then took one for himself and settled back in his chair. He blew on it, dispersing the rising steam while he obviously considered his words.

His eyes focused in on Melanie. "To answer your question from the other day, no. Not to my knowledge, at least. I discovered my…talent…by accident, and was fortunate enough to find a mentor while at the Academy. But it is not part of the general curriculum."

Melanie nodded slowly. "It must not be uncommon though, for you to find a mentor so easily."

"Hardly easily, but I take your point." Hamel took a sip of his tea and swallowed. "I cannot say whether it is common or not. It wasn't something I openly discussed with my classmates, at my mentor's urging."

"How is it you stay clear of the Magestirium's Inquisitors? If we could discover it, surely they must be aware of its existence as well."

Hamel waved a dismissive hand at her question. "I have no worry over them. There is a…dispensation…in the Magestirium's charter with the Crown."

Melanie blinked, and her eyebrows rose high on her forehead.

Hamel shook his head before she could ask the obvious question. "I will not discuss it, so don't ask. That is part of the arrangement."

"I…see…" Melanie was obviously intrigued, and perturbed at his refusal to talk about it. But if Julian knew her at all, she wouldn't just let it lie. Hamel may not speak of it, but that wouldn't stop her from pulling the string to discover the details, somehow.

"Tell us how it works," Raedrick said.

Hamel chuckled. "Still worried that I'm going to curse your town, or something?"

"Yes, actually," Julian said, and Hamel rolled his eyes.

"You've seen it yourself," Hamel said. "A little accentuation of the harmonies, a tweaking of the intended emotions of the song. It's an enhanced performance, nothing more."

"That's not what you did with Hab."

Hamel gave Julian a bemused look. "Of course it was." He set his teacup back down on the table. "Music stirs the soul, makes you feel how the composer wants you to feel from the structure of the song he wrote: the coordination of the notes, the tempo, the meter. If a good composer wants to make you cry, or laugh, you may cry or laugh, depending on the your emotional makeup, your mood, the time of day…a hundred different things. With my art, you *will* cry or laugh, as the composer intended. That's all."

Raedrick nodded. "They," he gestured toward Melanie and Julian, "felt the effects more strongly than I ever had when I've seen you play. And yesterday, Hab had a much more intense reaction than any of us."

"Well, of course everyone has a different emotional makeup. If someone is more naturally sensitive, or has some pent-up emotions he doesn't want to face," Hamel's eyes moved from Julian to Melanie and back, "he will be more susceptible. Yesterday, with Hab," he waved his hand in the direction of the fish warehouse, and got it pretty close, considering his short time in town so far. "He was already in a high state, and I put much more into it than I normally do."

"It didn't hit me as much as it had before," Julian said.

"But it did me," Raedrick added. "More than it ever had."

Hamel spread his hands. "It's not a precise art." He looked away, toward the stove in the corner, then a wry smile crossed his lips. "Perhaps this will help."

He leaned forward, matching Raedrick's pose. "A nobleman once asked me to help his son match up with the daughter of his rival. At first I thought it would be difficult, until I saw they were obviously attracted, but the rival's disapproval made the daughter hide it. And my employer's son was a bit too shy. So, at a ball, I played a ballad that was all about courage, facing the enemy, victory against immense odds, that sort of thing."

He grinned more broadly, and an amused twinkle came into his eyes. "It worked. My employer's son got up the nerve to ask her for a dance. But what I didn't anticipate is that it also encouraged everyone else, and one particularly arrogant pup cut in, quite rudely, putting his hands on her. The son is the sort that he ordinarily would have not protested much. But then, he did. The rude pup tried to fight him, and the son dealt with him handily."

Hamel's eyebrows rose. "That showing convinced the rival that the son wasn't so unworthy after all." He leaned back in his chair, spreading his hands again in a satisfied, almost beatific pose. "Worked like a charm."

"So you can't target a specific person," Raedrick said.

Hamel snorted. "Not unless you know a way to make one person hear music in a room while no one else does."

Julian supposed that made sense.

"The nobility knows of it?" Melanie said, sounding even more intrigued.

Hamel blinked, and flushed slightly. In his enjoyment of the story, he had let out more than he intended. But he regained his composure quickly, shaking his head. "Some do. I cannot say how many. I was surprised that man knew, but once he made it clear that he did, who was I to say no to his generous offer of employment?"

Which meant the nobleman, whoever he was, had Hamel over a barrel, or Julian was the Royal High Priest.

Raedrick pursed his lips thoughtfully. After a pause that seemed longer than it was, he said, "Well," and looked over at Melanie, then Julian. Melanie returned his look with a shallow nod. Julian's stubborn side wanted to continue objecting to what Hamel was doing, but he couldn't find a reason that didn't sound irrational, even to himself. He, too, nodded.

Raedrick returned their nods and looked back at Hamel. "I

think you've been here long enough that people know you, and appreciate having you around. Would you agree?"

Hamel nodded.

"And you clearly don't want your talents discussed widely."

"Just that one talent, Constable. My many others, I wish proclaimed far and wide!"

Julian couldn't help chuckling at that. Raedrick merely flashed a faint smile. "In that case, I would ask you to stop enhancing your performances from now on."

Hamel's lips turned downward at that.

"As you pointed out the other day, we're neighbors through the spring thaw regardless. And considering what you did yesterday…" He held his hand out to Hamel. "Keep up your end—don't cause any trouble or take advantage in that way—and we'll keep your secret for you."

Hamel paused for a moment, trying to look like he was mulling the offer over. But Julian considered they had him in almost the same position as that nobleman had. What was he going to do, say no? Considering the circumstances, Hamel didn't have much choice but to agree, did he?

Hamel clasped hands with Raedrick with a grin that again looked completely genuine and companionable. But this time, Julian didn't see that shadow as much as he had when they first stepped into the room.

"Agreed, Constable," Hamel said as he released Raedrick's hand. "And I thank you."

"I guess we should thank you, actually," Julian said, and leaned forward, best he could with his knee, holding his good hand out to him. "You made the situation with Hab come out better than it probably would have, otherwise."

Hamel's grip was not the most firm Julian had ever encountered, but it was good enough. "What else should I do for my town?" he said, and Julian chuckled along with him.

After all, it was true. Lydelton might not be his town forever. But at least for the moment, it was.

Hamel gestured toward the tea cups. "Well, now that that's taken care of, please don't let this go to waste. It's a blend from the lands east of Tyrash, and it wasn't easy to come by, let me tell you."

Julian didn't need any more encouragement. He picked up his teacup and took a sip.

It was pretty damn good.

28

OUT OF THE COLD

"You know he wasn't telling the whole truth, don't you?" Melanie asked.

They were seated at the closest table to the fireplaces in The Oarlock's common room that they could get. Both were lit, and filled with thick hunks of fuel that were burning merrily and giving off enough warmth to almost make Julian forget about the cold awaiting him just a few feet away, past the inn's thick entrance doors.

Almost.

They had come down after finishing their tea with Hamel, and decided to take lunch before braving the outdoors. So now they were awaiting their food as Raedrick nursed warm spiced wine, Melanie sipped from a goblet filled with dark-red, room temperature, wine, and Julian worked on a tankard of Winter's Folly that Mollie had somehow managed to coerce Holb into letting her sell to her patrons.

That must have been quite a negotiation. He wasn't entirely sure he would have wanted to see it.

Across the table from him, Raedrick took a sip and nodded.

Julian just shrugged. "Didn't expect anything else, really."

"And I'm not sure it matters," Raedrick said. "Even if he actually does means the town ill, and frankly I doubt that, unless he's a fool there's not much he can do about it until the spring. And he's no fool."

Melanie nodded slowly.

"Besides," Julian said, grinning at her as he reached out with his elbow to give her a nudge. "We all know you want him around."

She looked him askance, such that he thought she might actually be offended.

So he added quickly, "You're not going to rest until you figure out everything he didn't tell you about his magic. We all know that."

Melanie's expression mollified a bit. Just a bit. Then she nodded again, more briskly. "I *am* curious, especially about that dispensation he mentioned. If—" She cut off as Tami came up to their table, her tray laden with three bowls of Molli's signature spicy fish stew.

Tami laid their meal out, along with three cups of water and a hunk of bread, then got back about her rounds.

Julian didn't waste any time, tearing off a piece of bread and dipping it into his stew. "Something tells me by the time he leaves in the spring, you'll know more about his bard skills than he does." He bit off the soaked portion of his bread and chewed, relishing the rich flavor.

Melanie just shrugged and dug into her stew—with her spoon.

"That's assuming he leaves in the spring," Raedrick said.

Julian raised his eyebrows, and Raedrick shrugged. "We stayed. So did Jared."

"We had reason to."

"He may decide he has reason to as well."

Julian let that simmer in his mind for the time it took him to finish his bread dipping routine, then he picked up his spoon and waggled it at Raedrick. "I'll bet he moves on as soon as the passes clear."

"We'll see," Raedrick said. "Regardless, it can't hurt to keep an eye on him, in case he really is up to something." He chuckled. "Gods willing, we won't have all that much else to do until then."

Julian nodded emphatically. He'd already had enough action for one winter.

They ate in relative silence after that. Eventually, Julian came up from his now empty bowl and found that Raedrick had done the same. They looked at each other for a brief time, then Raedrick chuckled softly, and pushed his chair back.

"Well," he said. "I'd better check in on Lani and Celia before the afternoon rounds." He paused to place a couple coins down as payment for his meal. His gaze lingered on the coins for a bit, and he seemed to be chewing on something. Then he looked back up and Julian and Melanie.

"I was a little harsh with you two."

Julian blinked, surprised, and Melanie gave an emphatic shake of her head.

Raedrick raised his hand to forestall a response from them. "You were suspicious of Hamel and I tried to shut you down." He shook his head. "I should have been more quick to listen."

Julian shared a look with Melanie. "You didn't do anything wrong, Rae," he said.

"Yes, I did. If he actually *did* have ill intentions, he might have succeeded if I..." He sniffed softly, then continued, "It won't happen again." Raedrick straightened, almost coming to the position of attention. Then he nodded to them, and walked out of the inn.

The dim light of the snowy day silhouetted him briefly, a dark shape against the grey-white of the snowfall outside. Then the door closed behind him.

Julian looked back at Melanie, and she shrugged slightly but didn't say anything.

What was there to say? Julian hadn't felt affront from Raedrick's earlier doubt. Not really. And it had all worked out in the end. But he also understood what Raedrick meant. He had been similarly blind, toward Jared. Raedrick had extended his hand to Jared, while Julian had only wanted to cut it off, for what he did back in their army days. Cut if off, and then slit his throat for good measure.

It had taken several near brushes with death within the Falconer's Stairs to make Julian admit he had been wrong about Jared. Raedrick hadn't taken nearly that much to break through his stubborn side.

And anyway, he hadn't been wrong in the end, had he? Yes, Hamel had his own brand of magic, but had he really been up to anything nefarious? Julian couldn't honestly say yes to that. Hell, Hamel had actually saved their bacon yesterday. In a way.

As far as Julian was concerned, Raedrick had been right from the beginning.

Hard to tell that to his retreating back though, or to his stubborn hero demeanor, when he chose to don it.

Julian returned Melanie's shrug and grinned at her. "We'll have to make sure he remembers that, next time he think's he's right and we're wrong."

She rolled her eyes. "What do you mean, we?"

Julian could think of several times she had ended up being incorrect, but he decided to let the comment pass.

"I've been thinking," he said.

"Oh? Did it hurt your head?" she said sweetly, with not at all a bucket-full of teasing thrown into her tone.

Julian looked at her levelly for a second, then decided to let that slide as well.

"We need to talk about what's been going on here. No sense denying it anymore." He looked deeply into her eyes. "It's getting pretty cold out. All the time. I was hoping you could help me keep warm."

Melanie didn't flinch from his gaze. If anything, her eyes seemed to burrow into his.

Then she chuckled. "You want a brooch like I made for Raedrick, don't you?"

Julian nodded. "Damn right."

"I hate to break it to you, but I already looked into it and I don't have the components needed to complete a work like that."

"Well, there's got to be something you can do."

Melanie's mulled it over for a bit. Then her lips turned upward slightly. "I think I may have just the thing that will do the trick."

"Oh?"

She nodded, then sprang from her chair. "Come on. I'll show you."

She hurried over to the pegs beside the door and grabbed her cloak. Julian rose more slowly, and not just because of his knee. He looked at the coins Raedrick had left behind, then pulled out double that from his own purse and left them on the table alongside Raedrick's.

Whatever Melanie had in mind, it better be good, or she'd owe him for lunch.

MESSAGE FROM THE AUTHOR

Thank you for reading my book. I hope you enjoyed reading it as much as I enjoyed writing it.

Feel free to come say hi at my website, on Twitter, or on Gab. I always enjoy hearing from readers, especially since you all are, collectively, my boss.

Also, come check out my weekly podcast, Story Time With Michael Kingswood, where I read stories and talk through some of the latest goings on in my world.

Find it on YouTube, Rumble, Bitchute, Odysee, or through your favorite podcast feed.

Subscribers are always welcome, and encouraged!

Thanks again. My best to you and yours.

Warm Regards,
Michael Kingswood

MAILING LIST

If you enjoyed this book and would like word on new releases and special deals from Michael Kingswood, sign up for his newsletter on his website. Guaranteed to be spam-free, you can opt out at any time. And you can rest assured he will not share your information with anyone, for any reason, without a court order.

https://michaelkingswood.com/newsletter-signup/

ABOUT THE AUTHOR

Michael Kingswood has published more than 100 short stories, novellas, and novels. He has appeared in anthologies from WMG Publishing, Stark Press, and Knotted Road Press. A twenty year veteran of the US Navy's submarine force, he has four children and currently resides in San Diego.

Fans can contact him through his <u>website</u>, on <u>Twitter</u>, or on <u>Gab</u>.

Michael has a weekly podcast, Story Time With Michael Kingswood, where he reads his work and discusses writing, philosophy, and history. Subscribers are always welcome!

Listen on: <u>YouTube</u> <u>Rumble</u> <u>Bitchute</u> <u>Odysee</u> <u>Podcast</u>

MORE BOOKS BY MICHAEL KINGSWOOD

GLIMMER VALE CHRONICLES

Glimmer Vale

Out-Dweller

Tollard's Peak

Robbed Blind

The Falconer's Stairs

Campaign Season

STORIES FROM GLIMMER VALE

Legacy

Hidden Magic

Captive Hearts

Wedding Gifts

Lost Credit

THE PERICLES CONSPIRACY

Passing In The Night

The Pericles Conspiracy

SHORT FICTION

Michael has also published a number of shorter works, which can be found at michaelkingswood.com/store.